DEAD ANIMALS

DEAD ANIMALS

a collection of short stories and flash by

CS DeWILDT

Dead Animals
by CS DeWildt

First edition, August 2013. ISBN 978-0-615-86701-4.

Cover by Christopher Coffey. Book design by Julian Darius.

Stories in this collection have appeared in the following:
"A Bottle Room Can Save a Marriage" (*Visceral Uterus*, 2013)
"The Bull" (*Bartleby Snopes Issue 3*, 2009)
"Corbin's Dreams Take Flight" (*Literary Orphans*, 2013)
"Dig It?" (*Short, Fast, and Deadly*, 2012)
"A Glass of Water" (*Word Riot 2010*, online; reprinted in The Bicycle Review 2010)
"I Love the Devil" (*The Foundling Review*, online, 2010)
"In Love Like a Parvo Puppy" (*Dogzplot,* 2012)
"Love Among Apes" (Pure Slush: Notausgang, 2012)
"Pink Rubber Slivers" (*Foliate Oak*, online 2012)
"Pulp" (*52/250: A Year of Flash*, 2011)
"Shakespearian Variety" (*Criminal Class Press 6*, 2013)
"The Squirrel Hunter" (*Bartleby Snopes Vol 6*, 2010)
"That Boy Got Dynamite in His Hands" (*Eunoia Review*, online, 2012)
"To Bananas" (*A Clean, Well-Lighted Place*, print, 2012)
"To Sleep Well" (*This Zine Will Change Your Life*, online, 2012)
"The Tree House" (*Bartley Snopes: Post-Experimentalism, 2012*)
"Tu's Chicken" (*Bartleby Snopes*, online, 2009)
"The Yard Sale" (*Writer's Bloc*, online, 2010)
"You Just Never Know Where it's Been" (*Martian Lit* as "Just One Look," online, 2012)

Published by Martian Lit. For more information about this or other titles, visit martianlit.com.

for Justin and Chad

Contents

The Bull

"Get up, Jakey." The boy sat up in the bed. He smelled eggs. His breakfast. Five at five, every morning with a triple side of toast, no butter. The egg yolks stared back at him like yellow eyes. He stabbed the eyes with sharp toast corners and watched the goop flow. Jake inhaled the energy, ravenous with anticipation, not fear.

Dad put a large glass of water and a small glass of juice in front of him. Jake wiped up the last of the congealing yolk with his finger, ate it.

"When we leaving?" Jake said.

"Soon as you're done. Drink your water."

"I know." Jake lifted the glass and Dad stepped outside to smoke. He never smoked in the trailer because of the boy. He wanted nothing to harm him. That was one of the few truths he kept close.

Dad got out of prison when Jake was ten years old. He didn't even know about the boy. Jake was the product of a conjugal visit. His mom made it a pregnancy and then some before she saw Dad again. She told Dad the day before he was released. After she left, he sat alone in his cell, waiting for the doors to swing open the one last time. That was the longest day he'd spent there.

Jake washed his dishes by hand and put the dripping plate and cups into the drying rack next to the sink, next to the frying pan Dad had washed. At the door he pulled on his canvas sneakers. He ran a finger over the thin soles. They were worn smooth. Jake touched his face and felt the contrast of his scared, left cheek. It was a vivid remnant of the dog attack. Jake was five and he'd lost two teeth in the mauling. Now, seeing the scar, he decided he'd grow a beard when he could.

The dog was a stranger that had wandered onto the land, probably born in a barn and certainly more feral than pet. It took a piece of Jake and would have taken more, but Jake had the presence of mind to stick it in the belly with his pocketknife. The knife was Dad's, pearl-handled, though Jake had no idea. Jake had found it in an old toolbox under the stairs. That dog lay to rot in front of the trailer until the bloat was gone and the stink was too much. With a patched-up face and a bandana to block the dust and the stench, the boy dug a shallow grave and pushed the dog in with his foot. The dog's remaining skin and fur writhed with the undercurrents of flesh beetles and maggots. Jake watched and cocked his head left. Dropped in the knife. He filled the hole.

Dad killed his cigarette as Jake came out of the trailer. The eastern sky was just a little blue over the horizon. In the west the sky was still black and star filled. Jake looked over the yard. It was more of a field than a yard; there were no discernible boundaries, just brown dirt and rock and patches of overgrown mesquite. Old, waving saguaro cacti dotted the mountain foothills in the distance. There were no neighbors to speak of; there was the old man whose trailer could be seen as a tiny box a half-mile down the dirt road. There was no one to complain about the desert-dusted exercise equipment in front of the tin roof singlewide. Jake ran a finger over the silver weights resting heavy above the padded bench. He wouldn't lift today. He wouldn't ride the ancient exercise bike and he wouldn't pound the brown turf in his size 8s.

"Ready," Dad said.

"Yep."

* * *

Father and son sat like mirrored twins on opposing sides of the cool vinyl seat as the '79 Oldsmobile ate up the blacktop, their heads back, arms out the window, hands gliding on the wind. They drove west with the sun creeping up their backs. Jake felt they were trying to outrun the plasma ball and the feeling didn't bother him. It was old, familiar, like the dream he came back to often. When he thought about it, the dream, he couldn't remember if it was new or just freshly backdated. He told himself he would write down the date, keep a log so he would know when he had last remembered thinking about the dream. He never did it so it played out the same as before and Jake was left with nothing but a promise to himself to remember.

The news over the radio spoke of youth violence. Offenders were found to be getting younger, with teen girls being the group with the fastest rate of growth. Dad turned off the radio leaving only the wind and the cacti to entertain them.

"It isn't as bad out there as they'd have you think," Dad said.

"I know," Jake said.

"Do you?" Dad was looking at him and Jake felt it as he stared off into the Catalina mountain range to the north. He turned his head south.

"Yeah."

"Violence goes back to the gods."

"I know."

"Good."

It was bright and there was no denying the heat when they pulled into the Shell gas station. There was a white and green border patrol SUV parked out front. Next to it a flatbed full of Indians drank water and grain alcohol. There was a dog, black and gray, a blue merle herding mix, laying left of the entrance, panting. Its eyes were as bright as its ribs were visible. Jake watched it, resting his head on the car door while Dad pumped gas behind him.

"Dad, can I go see that dog?"

Dad looked turned from the scrolling numbers of the pump display, surveyed the lot.

"Alright, careful. You should eat something."

Jake doubled back, leaned through the open window of the Olds. He opened the glove box and grabbed the sandwich.

The dog watched Jake approach, saw something in the boy's hand, saw the boy looking at him, showing smiling teeth. The dog smelled the sandwich and its tail slapped the concrete.

"Hey boy." The dog stood slowly and stepped forward to meet the boy. Jake pulled the plastic bag from his sandwich and bit into it. He scratched the dog's head. Jake ripped away a piece of the sandwich. The dog took it gingerly, licking the tips of the boy's fingers.

"Good boy," Jake said. The dog smacked at the peanut butter stuck in its muzzle. They shared the rest of the sandwich equally.

"C'mon Jakey," Dad said exiting the store. Dad handed him a large bottle of water. Jake uncapped the bottle and poured a small stream, letting the dog lap at it. Jake took a long drink himself and then followed after Dad. He watched in the rearview mirror. The dog watched him go and then turned its attention to the evaporating wet patch of concrete next to the entrance.

They were sweating by afternoon and Jake climbed into the back of the car. He rolled down the back windows and climbed back into the front seat. He laid his head on the door, catching as much of the wind as he could.

"Stay hydrated," Dad said. Jake took a drink the water bottle. He lapped at the last falling drops and thought about the dog. He hoped it had a shady spot to sleep. Or a breeze.

Dad's ink was done in prison. He had a Nazi SS on his chest and a small swastika he kept covered with his wristwatch. One night, a while after Mom had left, there was a Nazi show on television.

"Do you hate Jewish people," Jake asked.

"No." Dad said.

"That's what your tattoos mean."

"I know."

Jake sat on the carpet of the trailer looking at his dad, waiting for an explanation. Dad drank the last of the warming beer from the can. "I'm gonna smoke," he said.

Jake sat alone in front of the TV in a mix of blue light from the screen and the yellow glow of the floor lamp next to Dad's chair. SS soldiers goose-stepped across the Sony Trinitron. With Dad gone the trailer felt big and the TV noise wasn't enough to calm the boy.

Jake stepped out of the trailer into the cool air. He sat down on the narrow trailer steps. Dad spoke to the night.

"Sometimes," he began, "you just do things because they're easier than fighting. Then they start to make sense because the rules aren't the same wherever you go. Whatever rules you got in your head, it don't always work that way. And to hell with making them understand."

Coyotes yelped and snarled out in the desert, miles away. Dad smoked one cigarette after another.

"Jakey," he said after a time. "You need to learn to fight."

The Olds burst a tire way out on Indian Road number 15. Jake stood by in the blazing noon sun sweating and watching his sweating dad, listening. There was nothing but open graze land in any direction, desert scrub for the cattle and donkeys and horses that wandered the landscape. There was another range of mountains further west. Jake didn't know what they were. Dad did, but it never came up.

"Loosen the lugs before you jack it up," Dad said. "Otherwise it's a real pain in the ass."

"Cause the wheel will turn?"

"Right." Dad said. He manhandled the L-shaped lug wrench and loosened four of the five nuts with the relative ease, the more stubborn of those yielded to gravity as Dad bounced his weight on the end of the tool. Teetering on one foot, hands holding the hood for balance, the fifth nut would not give.

"God damn, that bitch is on there. Get me the spare, Jakey."

Jakey pulled the bulky full- size spare from the trunk and rolled it through the dust to the front right quarter panel. The tire had been patched and plugged a million times and the tread was worn smooth as Jake's shoes. Dad lifted the tire and brought it down hard on the end of the lug wrench. The nut gave immediately.

"There we go," Dad said. Jake watched Dad jack up the car. There was the sound of an engine in the distance. Jake saw a vehicle, just a dot, come over the rise. It grew in size and volume quickly, roaring through the hot wavy air that glazed the road. The truck blazed by, kicking up dust. Jake turned his head from the stinging sand grains. He watched the truck shrink down again. It was the Indians from the Shell station. They shrank too.

"Think we got it. Put this in the trunk." Jake took the flat tire and pulled it to the back of the car. He heaved it into the trunk. Dad dropped the jack in next to it, slammed the trunk home.

"We late?" Jakey asked.

Dad wiped the grease and brake dust from his watch. "We're fine. Late doesn't apply to us, you know?"

"Yeah, I guess not."

As they drove away a fight-scarred coyote stepped onto the road and sniffed at the pair's fading scent. An automobile with working air conditioning would have left a condensation puddle behind. The coyote crossed the road and disappeared, blending into the landscape, searching on for sustenance.

Jake had not seen his mother since Dad came home. Jake knew him from old photographs. His favorite was a Polaroid of Dad standing shirtless in front of an old chopper. The bike was electric blue with a long thin fork, white and blue flame decorated the gas tank. Dad was smiling, holding a Budweiser can.

Dad came through the door of the trailer holding a blue gift-wrapped box Jake hoped was his. Jake's mom had dressed him in a suit and the tag from the shirt made his neck itch.

"Hi Jakey," Dad said.

"Hi Dad."

After dinner, Dad gave Jake the gift. He opened it carefully, not wanting to ruin the shining blue paper. Jake peeled the tape from one end and slid a box out of the decorative sheath.

"Monopoly, thanks."

"You ever play?" Dad asked.

"Yeah, but not on my own board. Will you play it with me?"

"Sure thing."

Dad and Jake sat together on the floor while Mom washed the dinner dishes.

Jake tore the cellophane wrapper from the box with less care than he had shown the wrapping paper. He opened the box, pulling out the various pieces: property deeds, red hotels and green houses, the dice, the pewter statuettes and the board.

"There's no money," Jake said.

"What?" Dad moved closer, scanned the contents, looked into the empty box. "Damn it, what a rip!"

"Did they forget?"

"I guess they did. Sorry Jakey. We can return it and get you a new one."

The Monopoly game was set aside and eventually found its way to the top shelf of Jake's closet. It never went back to the store. It was the kind of job for Mom, but she left in the night and neither had seen her since.

"Where'd she go?" Jake had said.

"Away," Dad said.

"For how long?"

"Forever probably." And that was the last they talked about her.

It was then the training started. Jake didn't have time to think about or miss his mom. Dad kept him busy with calm, disciplined training. Everything was routine. The eggs, the run, the bike, the bags. It began again at lunch, and then at dinner. There was no such thing as a day off.

"Prison put me on to a path I never would have known otherwise." Dad said sometimes as Jake sweat and panted. Jake listened intently because he never had a man tell him anything before.

The old farm was just off to the left before the road began to dissolve into a dirt 2-track and then raw desert. There were about 30 or so cars and trucks lined up in the dirt. Behind the old blockhouse a large group of men gathered. Jake saw the Indians from the truck mixed in with the rest of the men. More than 100 eyes found the Olds and the air was abuzz with a mix of Espanol, English, and tribal speak. The air smelled of testosterone and whiskey.

"Need a minute?" Dad asked. Jake thought.

"No."

Dad grabbed the black canvas bag from the back seat and set it between he and Jake. Jake unzipped it, pulled out the white tape. He peeled up an edge to get it started and handed it to Dad. Dad pulled a long piece of tape from the roll. Jake held out his right hand. Dad applied the tape while Jake fished through the bag among petroleum jelly, bandages, instant ice packs, and suture. He blew the dust from his red plastic mouth guard. When Dad finished with the right hand Jake gave him his left.

Dad took out a black marker and wrote "THE" on the taped right hand and "BULL" on his left.

The circular arrangement of the men at the old homestead was not of their own design. Jake approached, leading Dad, and the herd of men parted revealing the sectioned cattle gates. The metal gates were tied end-to-end with thick twine and arranged in a circle about thirty feet across. This is where someone had once worked their horses, breaking them and training them in the dust. At the far end of the circle stood a boy, maybe a bit older than Jake, bigger for sure. Jake looked at his own taped fists.

"El Toro," someone said.

Jake removed his shirt and pulled his lean frame through the bars of the gate. There was little fanfare, a few claps and whistles, but they were for the event, not the contenders. The boy across the circular ring bounced and stared at Jake. Jake met his gaze, held it. A small pregnant Mexican girl entered the space, stood center ring, blocking the fighters' view of one another. She held up a white board with the odds scribbled in red. Jake was the underdog at 13-1. Dad always put 100 dollars on Jakey, underdog or no. Jake looked at the Mexican girl, probably his age. Half of her face was fire scared and purple; the symmetry screamed intent. She turned in the ring and held the odds board high. Jake looked at her face as it rotated before him, one side flawless and beautiful, the other not so. She was partially bald and one ear was shriveled to a tiny lump of blackened cauliflower flesh. She exited the ring and the opponent was no longer staring, but talking to his corner, the lone man, probably the kid's dad. The referee entered. He was a little and old, brown and twisted like hot bacon.

Dad stood behind the gate, towel in one hand, water bottle in the other. "What are you going to do?"

"Get inside."

"When?"

"Immediately."

"Then?"

"Counter whatever he throws."

"And what'll that do?"

"Make him afraid to hit me."

"Right. Where's he look weak?"

Jake studied his opponent. The boy was like a man with an adolescent's head. His face was red with acne. He was well muscled and his torso was decorated with green, home-inked tattoos. Praying hands lay across his chest; tombstones and significant dates were placed randomly, faces of fallen ancestors, and on his neck, a baby's face and a single word beneath: AMORE.

"Nowhere."

"Ha. Everybody's weak somewhere. You find it and you keep on it."

"Okay."

"Don't worry about the odds. They don't know you. He's riding on his size. They think he's hard, but they don't know hard. He don't know hard. You're goin' to teach him hard. You hear me?"

"Yes."

"Say it."

"I'm hard. He's not."

"Good boy, Jakey. You keep on him."

A Mexican man struck the top bar of the metal gate with an 18-inch section of rebar. The sound was muted and thick.

"Get off the fence you dumb bastards!" the man yelled and three drunken men backed from the gate. The man struck the gate again, sending the tinny vibrations in all directions. He nodded, satisfied with the sound of the makeshift bell.

"Fight!" the grizzled ref commanded.

Jake lowered his chin and moved forward, staring past his own raised fists. He measured his opponent's reach and was ready for the jabs. Inside was Jake's place, always inside. He would suffocate the green trimmed man-child. The kid's punches were crisp and snapped Jake's head back. Jake pressed through the sting and kept on him. Another two quick jabs, pain, no noise anywhere. Jake continued to close the space. The size difference and the 1st few punches had the crowd counting their winnings.

"C'mon Jakey! Charge him! Charge him!" Dad said.

Jake didn't hear the words. They landed somewhere in his subconscious, but he did what was ordered through a combination of muscle memory and experience. He knocked away a jab, kept his feet moving and began throwing body shots in a furious left-right flurry. The tattooed boy hunkered down and brought his arms to his side to protect the ribs. Jake twisted his hard knuckles into the boy's arms at the end of each strike, trying to drill through the bone. He continued slugging at the body until the rhythm nearly became predictable. The man-child's arms dropped when Jake pressed ahead, not when he punched. Jake worked the body through another flurry and added a well-placed right uppercut. The kid stumbled back bringing gasps and cheers from the men around the ring. The kid's eyes went glassy for just a second. Jake pressed his advantage but the his opponent came back quickly, strong chinned and angry. A short exchange and a clinch. The ref pushed them apart and commanded they continue. The tattooed boy smiled at Jake, a show that he wasn't hurt, a sign that he had been.

Jake went back to work, driving inside the kid's reach advantage. He continued to pound the body, took more snapping jabs. Jake threw the uppercut several more times but couldn't land it cleanly, glancing them off of muscled shoulders or finding only empty space. He never stopped stalking. He took mean headshots and pressed forward landing hard shots of his own. The kid covered up his ribs. Jake threw a left hook that grazed the kid's chin. The kid stepped back, planted his feet and shot a straight right into Jake's solar plexus, right where the ribs opened up at the zyphoid process. The wind rushed out of Jake's body and his chest burned. He stepped back, slipping in the dirt. He stumbled, gasping. The tattooed boy stepped forward, pressed ahead.

"Get him! He's hurt!" Someone said through the garbled rush of voices. Jake's eyes focused beyond the boy. He saw the boy's smiling father. He saw the smile forming words: "Kill him! Kill him!" The mass of tattoos became his focus again. The right arm was cocked back at the kid's side. Jake allowed the fist to release and leaned back. He felt the wind of the powerful hook. The bell ended the round.

Jake went to Dad. He found air, breathed deep and came back to life. Jake tilted his head back and Dad poured water into his open, panting hole. He resisted the desire to take in the water. He swished it between his cheeks. He felt the contrast between his cool mouth and his sweating body. The sun was dipping toward the horizon but the heat would not relent. Jake spat in the dirt.

"Good round, Jakey. Keep the pressure on! Did he hurt you?"

"Just took my wind. I slipped."

"Did you find it?"

"He telegraphs his right hook big time."

"Good boy, Jakey. Now you make him pay for that. Keep working the body. That left feel good?"

"Yes."

"You know what to do then?"

"Yes."

The bellman struck the gate with his rebar. Dad slapped his shoulder and Jake pressed ahead.

"Yer dead, little boy," the tattooed boy said. His mouthpiece garbled the words, but his intent was clear, embedded in the tone.

Jake answered the threat with a burst of right hands. The last one caught the boy's floating ribs and Jake felt the crack, heard the squeal, saw the wince. Jake continued working the spot until he was caught with a solid hook that made him see the familiar flash of white. He answered with his own powerful right cross and went back to the ribs before the kid's head could face him again. The kid began to circle; Jake stepped with him, cutting off the escape. The kid changed direction and Jake followed, slicing the ring further. He pressed on. The kid stepped forward and landed some hard body shots. Jake threw a straight right and found the empty space left by a tilt of the head. The boy landed a clean left to Jake's temple. The flash returned; Jake's legs gave. He went down to the dirt.

"...3...4...5," the ref counted. Jake felt the hot sand on his cheek. The men surrounding the ring were going apeshit crazy. Jake saw the tattooed boy at his corner, two of him. The boy's father was slapping his back, raising his arm.

"C'mon Jakey! Get up!"

"7...8" the ref shouted. Jake swayed as the world settled, six physical dimensions coalescing to three. The ref blocked his path, took his hands. "Are you okay?"

"Yes."

"Look me in the eye," the ref ordered. Jake did it. He forced his swollen lids open and stared into the ref's face.

"I'm fine. I'm fine."

The ref nodded. He returned to a neutral space between the boys.

"Fight!"

Jake charged. He would never stop crowding the man-child. The kid met him, sensing an advantage. He launched a power shot that Jake dodged easily. Jake countered with a hard straight right that broke the boy's nose. Jake almost laughed at the crooked beak in front of him, until the red blood began to flow. The boy opened his mouth, unable to breath otherwise. His eyes watered and his chin hung loose below the hole. Jake watched the blood stream from the nose and drip off the chin, the drops slapping home in the dirty blood puddle. Jake felt the anger begin to creep in. He harnessed it, charged. Jake launched wild body shots, tucked his chin. He tightened his core. The straight right to the body came again and landed in the same spot it had in the 1st round. Jake kept his air, but stumbled back. The kid's fist was already cocked at his side as he stepped forward, bloody and angry.

Jake slid his left foot back into a southpaw stance and drew out the earth's power through his leg. The kid's father was screaming. "Watch the left!" The man yelled. The boy's right fist stayed low. He moved closer, shaking it, ready to unload.

Jake measured the distance and dug into the dirt with his feet. The energy flowed up his legs, through the twist of his hips, through his shoulder, his arm. The twisting fist landed hard underneath the kid's open chin, slamming his teeth together. He bit through his tongue and Jake punched through the boy. He imagined the kid's face giving in, collapsing. Jake could feel the soft and hard tissues, hot and moist. He drove through brain matter and lifted the kid from the planet as his fist met the inside of the skull.

The man-child did not get up by his own power and the payouts were made. Jake and Dad cleared close to three grand from the purse and the bet. Dad put his arm around Jake and held him tight and close as they walked back to the Olds. Hard, stinging, congratulatory hands landed on Jake's back. "El Toro" became a mantra.

"Thank you," Jake said. "Thank you." Jake looked among the men for the burned girl. She was not there.

Dad drove through the dark. It was quiet except for the cool desert air rushing over the car and the rumble of the engine. Jake's body was tight and sore. His face was swollen. His head throbbed.

"You done good, kid." Dad said without looking from the road.

"I know." Jake said. Now Dad looked at him.

"Good," he said. "Your face hurt?"

"Not too bad."

"Well, it's killing me."

The laugh shook his torso and Jake winced. He leaned against the car door and felt the cool glass on his hot, tender face. He closed his eyes.

Jake thought about the dog from the Shell station. He wondered what had become of it. He saw himself and the dog in the back the Olds. The dog loved him; this boy who pried swollen red ticks from his flesh and dropped them out the window into the night. After a time he could ignore the pain. He slept.

Bad Habits

Gus sat on the dented hood of his '79 Camaro, fishing pole across his lap, but there'd be no fishing. Sheriff Davey Poll had the pond under investigation. Seems someone had drowned down there. How you could drown in that pond was a mystery to Gus and he resented the dead man for screwing up his nightly ritual.

Gus had a view of the entire scene from atop the hill, in the parking lot of the dead and boarded Shell filling station. There was an ambulance to take the guy away when they finally found him. The paramedics' initial fervor had boiled away and now they leaned motionless on the front of their vehicle, waiting, arms crossed, watching the water. Davey did the same on the front of his cruiser and all three men perked up a little less each time the diver surfaced to tell them he hadn't found a body. Apart from the men, a young girl, no more than eleven or twelve, was playing in the gravelly sand, her floral print towel tied around her neck like a cape. She wore a peach colored one-piece swimsuit. Gus felt like hollering down to that fat lard Davey Poll, that worthless SOB, to tell him he should give it up, pack it in and get back to his speed trap. Gus suspected the diver worked by the hour, probably found the guy first time he went down and wanted to milk the clock.

No one spoke to the girl, but then she didn't appear to need any kind of comforting. Gus watched her watch her own feet as she kicked around sand the shoreline. She was making small hills with bulldozer feet, dozens of them, before turning from creator to destroyer and stomping them flat. She seemed as unconcerned as the rest of them standing at the water and Gus wondered who the man in the pond was to her.

He waited another fifteen minutes and still no change at the pond. Gus hopped from his car started toward the pond. He skirted the top of the hill that wrapped the pond, stepped into the thin secondary growth that separated the property line of the gas station from the city property that included the pond. Behind the far bank, he could see the cars slow on the M-45, speeding up again as their driver's necks snapped back to shape.

He waded through the brush and saplings, stopped twice to unhook his line from the small branches before leading with it to avoid another hang up. He came out of the trees and stood on the narrow bank opposite the action. He cast his line and the buzz of the reel drew the eyes of the men and the girl. The men dismissed him, but the girl stopped her stomping game to watch. Gus lit a cigarette and sunk his backside into the cool sand, watched the orange and yellow bobber settle among its own ripples. He sat on guard, waited for Davey to holler at him the way he did to the kids at the high school football games or at the Country Sundae ice cream stand when they were just hanging around doing nothing. Davey was only a few years older than Gus, but Davey's dad owned a car dealership and was supposed to be something big in town, bowled with the mayor for the city team in the Tuesday league. The mayor even campaigned for Davey when the latter decided he should be elected sheriff. Gus remembered Davey's fat ass on the back of the Cadillac convertible during the Salad Days parade, waving and throwing handfuls of Hershey's miniatures, the Special Darks and Goodbars anyway. He'd saved the Krackles and regular Hersheys for himself, leaving a trail of red and brown wrappers behind the car like ticker tape.

"No fish in here," she said and the start she gave him nearly sent Gus into the pond. She stood still with her knees together, watching the idle bobber.

"There is too," Gus said.

"Ever caught one?"

"Sure, plenty."

"No you haven't. I know for a fact that there's not a single fish in there. Water's too polluted, pesticide runoff and all that. And I bet money the gas tanks they got buried up there leak."

"You don't know that," Gus said, forgetting that there was a dead man in the water and that he might belong to her. "I caught eighteen bluegills here just last week. Ate them too and they didn't taste polluted."

"You show me when you catch a fish then and prove me wrong. I bet you didn't catch anything. Except for cancer from eating those nasty fish."

"Ha. You're going to go broke with all that betting. And if I do get cancer from the fish that means I must have caught one."

She rolled her eyes, but said no more about it. Gus turned back to his pole and he considered how right she was. He had never caught a fish- at the pond or anywhere else- and she was probably right about the pollution too. He huffed. Now the whole exercise was nothing but a pathetic farce meant to show up a little kid. He looked out over the water again, to Sheriff Davey who had finally noticed the girl's absence and was looking at her and Gus. Gus met his eyes and the fat man offered no sign of recognition, no public servant cordiality. Gus finally broke the gaze and turned to the girl. Her legs were in his face, sun darkened and at contrast with the peach of the swimsuit. The stems were skinny and the skin was smooth aside from the razor nicks, fresh as if she'd recently shaved for the first time. Overlooked, stray blonde hairs accented the legs like the thin stand of trees behind the rest of her.

"What's going on over there?" Gus finally asked.

"They're looking for my daddy."

"Oh." Gus waited for more, but the girl offered nothing. She began making sand piles with her feet. "He's in the water?"

"Nope."

"So what's that guy in the scuba suit looking for?"

"They think that's where he is. But he isn't."

"Why'd they even think to look there then?"

"There was some people here when he went in, fishing like you, didn't catch a thing. I guess they called the ambulance."

"So he's not in the water?"

"You deaf? I said he isn't."

"So where is he?"

"I can't tell you."

Gus nodded toward the men on the opposite bank. "You tell them he wasn't in the water?"

"They didn't ask me. They said, 'Rinthy, your dad go in there?' I told them he did. 'Cause, he did."

Gus looked at Davey and smiled. He suddenly liked the kid. He liked anybody that could make Davey's life difficult, even a little bit.

Gus watched the bobber, still doing nothing. Rinthy continued her sand game. He listened to her grunt, a mix of pain and satisfaction as she demolished every pile she built. Gus thought to ask her about the game, but it put him at ease- this young girl playing next to him- and he didn't want to interrupt it. Plus he figured that if he did ask he'd just get some half answer leading to more questions than he felt like asking. Eventually, after at least one hundred of her grunts, she became quiet and sat next to him, closer than was comfortable. It puzzled him that the proximity of this little girl could make him so ill at ease.

"What you using for bait?" she asked.

"Can't tell you. It's a secret."

"Bet you're using earthworms."

"There you go again. And I'm not. You'll never guess in a million years."

"So tell me then," Rinthy said. Gus shook his head. He stalled the issue by pulling out a red package of cigarettes, shook it upward to produce a single brown filter and brought the pack to his mouth. He pulled out his red disposable Bic and lit fire to the end of the cigarette, sucked deep.

"Can I get one of those?" Rinthy said.

"Yeah right. You think I'm going to contribute to your delinquency? How old are you anyway? Ten?"

"I'll be thirteen next month and I smoked before. Dad lets me smoke all the time."

"Really?"

"Yep. Said I was going to start sometime so it might as well it be now, with him. Said it made me look more grown." She licked her lips. "So can I have one?"

Gus thought on her words and looked again at the cuts on her legs before making sure Davey wasn't watching him. The sheriff was sitting in his cruiser, talking into the radio.

"I guess if Dad says okay." Gus dropped his own burning cigarette onto sand and let Rinthy help herself to it, absolution by technicality. He lit a fresh one for himself.

"So what you use for bait?"

"I told you, it's secret."

She stood and held up the cigarette. "You better tell me or I'm going to tell the sheriff you gave me this." Gus didn't know if she was joking or crazy or what. She looked at him with cold eyes and if she *was* joking she had a deadpan to convince God himself.

"Calm down. I'll tell you." He looked away from her, at the bobber. "I don't use anything. I don't use bait."

"You don't use bait?"

"That's what I said."

"Well why not? How you supposed to catch anything? I knew you never caught any fish in here!"

"I told you I caught plenty. It's just- I don't know- it just never seemed right to me, tricking the fish. You know? Offering them something they want and then giving them a hook through the mouth." He shrugged and looked across the pond. "When I catch a fish it's because that's what it wants."

Rinthy looked at the bobber on the water and back at Gus. She put the cigarette to her lips and put her backside back in the impressions next to him. She coughed and then didn't pull from the cigarette again. She stared ahead, watching the men, or the bobber, or maybe the just the water.

"You want to know about my daddy?" she asked.

Gus shrugged. "If you feel like telling me."

"He's the devil."

"Huh? What's that mean?"

"Said the hole to hell is at the bottom of this pond and that's where he was going. Back home. That's why they can't find him in there."

Gus watched the girl in profile. He wondered if she if she might really be touched in the head.

She leaned forward and tapped at her cigarette over the edge of the water. The ash fell away and hit the water with a hiss.

She held the cigarette to Gus. "I don't want this." The boy took the smoke and put it between his fingers with the other one. He held the pole out to her.

"You want to try?" He asked.

"'Kay." She took up the pole and they sat quiet for a long time, just watching the bobber. "You really never tried to bait the fish?" she asked.

"Nope."

"So if we catch one that'll really be something, huh?"

"Yep. I think so."

The diver came up again and said something to the men on the shore. He waddled out of the water like some kind of duck man on giant webbed feet.

"What the hell you talking about?" Davey said. "He's down there! Where's he gonna go? Huh? Tell me that, you moron!" Gus and Rinthy watched Davey as he paced on what to do next, searching for the answer on the tops of his shoes. Then he raised his head, looked across the pond and made his way toward them.

"You gonna to tell him that your daddy isn't there?"

"If he asks me I guess I will."

Davey came around to their side of the pond, wiped a line of sweat from his brow with his shirt sleeve. "Girl," he said. "This is taking some time. You got family we can call?"

"None close by. My mom's in Kentucky, I think." She kept her eyes on the bobber as if keeping vigil. The sky was getting purple and the orange and yellow plastic was muted gray by shadow.

"I'll have to call in someone from the county then. And you need to go," he said to Gus. "This isn't the time to fish. No fish in here anyway."

"He's caught plenty," Rinthy said. "Don't even have to use bait."

"No bait? That what he told you? He'd a goddamned liar this one is. Or stupid. Ha!"

Gus looked up at the man. "Too stupid to find a man at the bottom of a pond? Or maybe just too fat. Maybe if my dad was friends with the mayor I could catch a fish."

Davey stepped over the fishing pole and booted at Gus's legs. "Get up you little sonnabitch." Gus crab walked backward and got to his feet. Davey had a fist cocked at the ready.

"I got one. I got one!" Rinthy said. Gus and Davey watched as the end of the pole bent under the weight of the catch. She cranked the reel and the line froze. She pulled the whole rod. "It's a big one!"

Davey moved in next to her. "You're gonna snap the line doin' it like that. Feed it some slack!"

Gus watched them standing at the edge of the pond, Rinthy's skinny brown legs, Davey's backside just begging for a boot, the bobber gone.

Shakespearian Variety

The one I think about most is my Michelle. I watch her every day from my desk, stalking, hidden behind piles of neglected grading. My first post grad gig and I'm already jaded. I ask her: "You heard that Beatles song, 'Michelle'?"

"Who the hell are The Beatles?" she says. Fucking high school girls. She goes back to balancing equations; the assignment was due a week ago. I think about telling her to wise up on the music, listen to something other than whatever noise it is drilling her skull from the ipod. Then I just think about drilling her skull. She's sex. Tiny and breakable if you bend her far enough, but she's tough and bending her to that point, it's not a given. I saw how she got the ipod. It fell from the hoodie pocket of the girl she jumped and stomped after school. It's pink and only suits her if you don't know her. She's that kind of cute. She wears shirts that show off tits and she doesn't care who eyes her. I see no panty lines, just crack under her tramp stamp. I don't hold that trendy ink against her. She's young. I think about locking myself in the faculty bathroom and rubbing one out, seeing her on her knees, cupping me and lapping me like a sweet dog. Then I lift her off the dirty floor and she wraps her legs around me and I'm wet and she's wet and—

"Mr. D., how do you do this again?" It's Corby. He's an idiot, but I guess that's why I'm there. I tuck away my nice little distraction and let myself deflate.

"It's like this," I say, pointing to the problem. "It's like this."

I hang back in the schoolyard and let the kids talk and smoke. I have my shades on so the girls can't see my eyes looking them over, wanting them. I like how new they are, just out of the package and ready for damage. I like Michelle the most. I want to make her know it.

She's talking to the fat girl, telling her that Daddy won't let her out this weekend. Oh, if I was Daddy I wouldn't let her out either. I'd protect her good. But I'm not and her words get me to thinking, thinking about braining daddy with something blunt.

They took her car away again so I hang around after school, get her in the hall

"Want a ride?" I say. She does but only if I can take the fat girl too. C'mon fat girl.

"Wanna smoke some hash?" I say. She looks at me but I have my shades on and she can't see what's really on my mind, looking down at her. She thinks I'm square as they come, scientist, teacher. She wants to be surprised but knows if she acts fazed she'll be out of character.

"You got hash?"

"I got hash," I say, nodding to the glove box. She pulls out the baggie and breaks off a nice chunk of the blonde and puts it into her own purple piece. It's got raised metal butterflies on it. I fall in love with her for the thirteenth time that day. We pass it around, toke up all the way to her house way over on the south side. Michelle rests her head on her arms, head out the window like some beautiful dog. She's watching the Rincon mountains sprout over the top the Tucson concrete valley, longing to run free among the giant saguaros.

I plant seeds. I tell them stories of my youth, getting drunk and plugging those cacti full of gun powder and watching them explode, hiding from the border patrol in a wash full of rattlers. I tell them how lucky they are, reinforce the fact that any generation but their own is wrong, and no other generation will ever be as right. I tell them to be cool, keep quiet about this. I tell them I have more of whatever they want. I tell Michelle this. Fat girl is just there giving my struts a workout.

I stretch out the yellow light "just a few blocks away" from her house. The cruiser chirps and flashes its lights. I'm sweating because I'm human. I hide it because I'm cool.

"Stash the shit," I say cracking the windows. I pull to the side of the road and Michelle crotches the shit, mine and hers. I hear her squeal and gasp and a tear wants to jump, but she keeps it on the ledge.

"Be cool."

The officer's got a nose like a hound gets and gets us out of the car. I let him search. He's got the brain of a hound too, pats us down, doesn't find shit. He gives me a ticket for running the red and sends us on our way. He follows us to see if I'm on the level.

"Just giving a couple of my students a ride home, Officer."

I drop them both at Michelle's. Michelle lays her hand over mine as it vibrates on the chrome skull shifter.

"Thanks," she says and let's her fingers run the length of my own before looking to the house, to fat girl waiting to go inside.

Michelle winks. "She's got the munchies."

* * *

I'm alone in my apartment before I realize she's still got my hash in her pants. In the shower I touch myself and curse her name and pop her in the mouth before she begs...

"fuck me...fuck me...fuck me..."

And I do.

I step out of the shower and I can hear her purple nail polish through the door as she taps. I finish drying myself, dress and open up the door. I say something cordial like, "What brings you here?"

She stands at the threshold. Am I mentor or friend?

I'm neither.

We smoke and she sits next to me on the couch. We watch cartoons and laugh out loud. I savor her kiss and bite her lip and she squeals like she did in the car. She touches me and I'm in the kind of heaven you burn in. I carry her to my bedroom. She's so light. I drop her on my bed and she bounces. She peels off her jeans and I was right about the panties. I see the raised butterfly blister next to her landscaping.

"It hurts," she says, teasing it with her finger.

"Let Daddy kiss it."

"I listened to that song." She moans. "You're sweet."

I could cry. The finest moment a teacher can have is getting through to a student.

I feel relief and release and guilt. And the guilt can only be assuaged by her hands on me. She digs her purple nails into my ass and pulls me toward her and what Nietzsche said is true: the only way to rid of temptation is to give into it.

Or maybe it's more like shooting a bad dog. You could lock the dog up, chain it to a tree, but it's still a bad dog. Shoot it and it's a problem solved, even if it comes back an undead beast more fearsome than before.

She's hungry and wants lo mein.

"I know a place."

I walk alone in the night. The cool desert breeze has cleared away the last of my sweat and sex as I step into the restaurant.

"*Ni Hao.*"

"One shrimp lo mein. One eggroll." One lo mein is enough for two. One eggroll means you get two. I know my paper fortune says *what's vice today may be virtue tomorrow.* I'll put it in the little slot under my doorbell, where my name should be.

Michelle eats and the noodles dangle, she bites them and lets them fall and her face is blue, lit up by the television in the darkness of my apartment. She watches the man on the screen. I watch her. She feeds me eggroll. She's what I wanted and what I want. It's a rare combination. Like pork stir fry and sesame chicken.

I ask her to stay and she says: "Can't, Daddy".

I ask her to come back tomorrow and she says: "Can't Daddy". I crack open my cookie and my fortune says that I am lucky in pursuits of the heart.

I drive her home and smell her and the scent mingles with the sex. She bites my neck and giggles and we are both sixteen for the rest of the drive. We share a milkshake at Sonic. She says I was too nice to the girl on skates.

"She reminds me of you. I wish everyone in the world was you."

"You can't leave me now. I know your secret."

"I'll tell you another one," I say. I pull the cherry from the whipped cream and tell her to hold it between her teeth.

"Just hold it. Don't bite it. Hold it."

I punch her in the mouth.

"I knew it," I say.

"Knew what?" She's trying not to cry.

"That your blood was the color of cherries."

"Did you hurt your hand?" She kisses my fist, bleeds on the knuckles that busted her lip. We kiss and share the chocolate and cherry and blood.

"I have to get home."

"All right."

We drive in silence. I listen as she slurps the remainder of the frozen treat. It's dark. There's rain. Distant headlights grow, from seed to full bloom they rise and fall like spirits on leave. I like the way they wash her over and I know they wash me over too, but I don't think it's the same kind of thing I'm seeing right now. She smiles and there's only a little blood on her lip and I want to kiss it better.

"You ever just want to hit one of them?"

"Who?" I say.

"The other cars, swerve and take them out?"

"Who hasn't?"

"Do it?"

"Okay."

I grip the wheel as my head sponge tries its best to preserve itself and stop me from being stupid. If my own mind believes it, she must believe it. She tenses up despite herself, like my mind, and I believe in her fear. I jerk my hands hard left, but let them slip over the smooth wheel.

"Oh shit. We just destroyed the all-American family." I say. "Decapitated the mother. Deboditated the father."

"And the kids are still watching their DVD."

We laugh and wish it was real.

"You're such a pussy," she says.

"I know. I know. I know."

The Squirrel Hunter

He followed Everett through the hills and hollers, down steep limestone embankments of clacking rocks that served as the path for the heavy rain that would spill out into the flood plains below. He followed the man through patches of paw-paws and young birch, past old hollow oaks that vibrated with huddled bats in wait of dusk, up the next rise where their heavy breath flattened the land again, leading them among primordial ferns and moss-pillowed stone.

Everett carried the twenty-two rifle in his giant mitts. Breath came like smoke and the man chewed the end of his home-rolled cigar. Billy watched him and the man seemed to him like a silver haired bear. The man would often stop and talk of the plants, to Billy, but also to the air itself, spilling the words for the forest to gather unto itself, as if educating the very place on its true nature.

"These are wild onions," he said squatting, knees popping like the rocks. He pulled up the thin scallion and chewed the bulbous root. Billy did the same and sucked the flavor from the green fiber. He chewed the sprout, letting it dangle from his lips like Everett's cigar.

"These berries are edible," Everett said. "I don't care for them myself, bitter. But in a pinch." And he plucked two from the small bush and popped them as if to prove the point. Billy did the same and yes, they were bitter, but they complimented the onion flavor and Billy memorized the look of the bush, the stubborn give of the berry's skin between his molars.

It was cold and the ground spouted forth smoky steam from the pockets and caverns below. Billy pointed out each breathing hole he saw and Everett marked its location on the topographical map.

"Most of these are connected. Or will be." Everett said. "Might just open up into some great chamber. A place untouched."

Billy noted the marks on the map, simple red exes laid out over the paper landscape, each one a ghost of the vents pocking the land around them.

Everett paused and Billy knew he'd spotted a squirrel by the change of his breathing, a feeling in the air as if the man had sucked up all the oxygen in some great ecological communication as master of the world. Billy massaged the canvas bag between his fingers, wanting the moment to remain with him in all its manifestations, tactile and olfactory. He smelled the cigar on the onion on the berry on the cold morning. He saw the man take a knee, another pop of the joint, a click of the safety next to the trigger, the pop and soft echo from thick greenery. It fell from the tree, hobbled, bounced and flopped, became a gray mass.

Billy came upon it first, went to his knees and spread the frosted ferns that wet his fingers numb. The squirrel did not appear. Billy cocked his head like a robin searching out the slow crawl of a worm and in doing so the gray mass popped from the rocky background, burning itself upon his retinas. He felt the squirrel, the warm radiating death soothed his cold fingers. The tick, a young instar was slightly swollen behind the squirrel's ear. Billy plucked it free, a small tag of flesh still in its mouthparts. He rolled it in his fingers before crushing it, slicing it in two between his thumbnail and the hardened bed of his index finger. It bled squirrel blood and fell to the ground, left to new purpose among the miraculous and unseen perpetuators of the cycle.

The squirrel moved, barely, and Billy thought it still alive. There was a hole in its midsection and Billy realized the pulsing was not due to the animal's blood flow or breath, but to squirming life within its womb. The bullet had opened up the placenta and among the messy potpourri of innards and fluids, a small wet pup was exposed to the world prematurely. Billy watched it move and take life upon itself the best it was able, the cold invasive air, light and sound. It searched for the comfort that had been stripped away with the layers of tissue.

He felt Everett over his shoulder, smelled the cigar and felt his breath. It warmed his neck and Billy said, "Will it live?"

"No," Everett said. "It won't."

Billy took the squirrel by the bush of its tail and dropped it into the bag among the others. Everett marked the map with another double stroke of red and Billy scanned the landscape, searching for the place his father had just created.

Love Among Apes

Delusory parasitosis is a condition in which the host believes he is infested with bugs. It can manifest itself in everyone; try not to acknowledge the itch when someone says "head lice."

Extreme cases include people who feel the bugs at all times. Ridiculed, labeled "crazy", or "weirdo", they're told it's in their head. Maybe the others, but it wasn't in *my* head.

I scratched my face raw that morning. I looked into the mirror and saw the red swelling through my patchy beard. I felt the glorious burn as skin flaked free from my cheeks and chin and neck. I told myself to stop it. Cut it out. I scratched.

The medical types, they all referred me to the same support group. One week, sitting in the circle, listening to the share, I picked and bled so bad they stopped the meeting and sent me packing with a handful of thin, smooth napkins from the coffee station. Outside, alone in the night I stuck the napkins to my bleeding face and walked home, cursing the bastards to everyone I met on the way.

* * *

I pulled a strip of clear tape free from the roll and stuck it flat to my cheek, ripped it off. I saw the flakes of skin and a little blood, coarse beard hairs. I saw the tiny black specks. Feces? Eggs? They could not be missed. I got off the bus with the tape folded over in my pocket, a clear rectangular slide to be examined.

"What is it?" I asked Professor Philips. He stared through the eyes of the stereomicroscope, adjusting focus, the magnification. The shelves around us were packed tight with vials of bugs in sweet smelling ethyl alcohol, boxes of mounted specimens pinned through the thorax, preserved with mothballs against the scavengers. They watched us.

"It's nothing. Like always, it's nothing. Now leave me alone, please!"

I stepped from his office, defeated again, but then he called me back. He saw them! I leaned into his doorway, scratched my chin.

"If you contact me again," he said. "I'm calling the police."

* * *

I followed her from the campus at a distance. I'm sure she didn't notice. She stepped lightly in heavy combat-style boots. She disappeared into a crowd of waiting pedestrians, I picked at my face and arms. My feet began to itch and I rubbed the raw surfaces against the inside of my sandpaper-lined shoes. Her glow reappeared as she separated from the crowd and crossed the street. I let the blood and venom dry into my shirtsleeves.

She entered the zoo and I followed, placing my feet where hers had been. She paused at the llama enclosure, watched as the matted beast spat cud into the face of a teenage boy who'd moved too close. I stood still, exposed, but she did not see me, her gaze diverted by the laughter of the boy's companions. We continued.

She stripped off her purple backpack in stride, smoothly, as if disrobing, and pulled a notebook from the pack's depths. She came to rest on a bench adjacent to the largest single piece of glass in the zoo. The chimpanzees sat inside the enclosure, each space chosen by rank and force. The old male sat graying, looking indifferent in his swinging rope chair.

"Hi Sammy," she said to him.

Two juveniles played on the sunken floor below, yanking on one another, stealing, tugging ropes, snacking on the undigested roughage from their feces.

I walked to the glass and pretended to ignore her, though I was able to steal glances at her face from the glass itself, framed between the bolts and welds. I watched the old male look at her, and she at him in a single field. I longed to steal her attention.

"What's with the notebook?"

She looked at me. "Research."

I waited. She wrote. Two females slept in the rope vines. Young adults lay far below, in the pit of the enclosure.

She read my face. "It's a comparative study. I'm observing the differences in behavior between confined and free chimps. It's my last day of data collection on these captives."

I nodded and scratched and wished I'd washed my hair.

"Are you itchy? You got bugs?"

"Yes. Yes I have. They say it's in my head, but they're wrong. They're under the skin, hard to catch. I think the air liquefies them or something."

"Does the picking help?"

"It's all I can do."

She looked into the glass. Sammy looked at her with brown, almost-human eyes. He was balding, withdrawn, and I knew she saw a father in him.

"If we were chimps you'd have someone to pick at the bugs for you. How would you describe their demeanor?"

"Huh?"

"Right now. I want to compare your opinion to my data."

I looked past her reflection, into the enclosure.

"Lethargic, bored maybe."

"I agree. My prelim data analysis suggests that these chimps are in a depressive state, brought on by captivity."

She put her palm to the glass. Sammy watched as she drummed her knuckles on the pane.

"I'm a scientist. Student ethologist technically. Master's candidate."

"Sure."

"You know what that is? Ethology?"

I started to itch again. I dug my nails into the back of my neck. "Like a behaviorist," I said.

She looked back to Sammy and then to me again. I ground my thumb knuckle into my eyelid.

"Tired?" she said.

"I don't sleep much."

"Well you better wake up." She placed the notebook in the pack and replaced it with a nickel-plated hand cannon. I thought she was going to put me out of my misery until she approached the enclosure and began unloading round after round into the reinforced glass. The chimps scattered with teeth bared as they clambered up the trees, their angry shrieks reverberating fear inside.

A man in a red flannel jacket - bearded and rugged, brawny like that paper towel guy - approached us with a long confident stride I envied. I watched him slap three gray gobs of clay to the glass and then affix detonators.

The girl pulled me by the arm and I felt complete relief as I surrendered to her will. I stumbled along, tripping over my own feet, straining to watch the pandemonium behind the spider-cracked glass. The lumberjack caught up to us and they slid their arms around each other. And the girl wasn't pulling me anymore.

I heard the bombs explode and felt the ground shake, waking the crawlies and bringing the itch to the soles of my feet. I turned back again, tasted the smoky tang in the air. I heard chimpanzees' primal hoots- or maybe it was the liberators- as the black smoke plumed above and the panic grew, spilling like lava, an angry, rumbling chaos poised to burn everything.

They hopped the turnstiles and I called to her: "I would have done this for you! Why couldn't I have met you first?" And then she was gone. Behind me I heard the screams, the trampling feet, the shrieks of the chimpanzees. I felt the mass of people swallow me, a single swollen body too massive for the exit. I pulled the specimen slide from my pocket, held it steady in front of my face. They were right there. How could they not see the bugs?

My tears flowed and I dug my nails into both cheeks, deep, touching my fuzzy teeth. God damn, did I itch.

A Favor Returned

He cranked the steering wheel hard left as he went off the road. The car slid sideways down the bank, hit the bottom of the ditch hard. The Honda was good in the snow, but no way he was getting it out as easy as he'd put it in. The young man killed the engine, got out and scrambled up the embankment, back up to the road.

He wore a light jacket, no gloves or hat. He'd read a story once about a guy in Alaska who got wet and froze solid before he could get a fire lit. There was a dog, a wolf dog that the guy tried to kill for warmth. The story ended and the dog was fine. West Michigan in December was not Alaska, but it was snowing and he needed to find some help.

He walked up the long driveway in the dark. There were lights on in the little farm house. He knocked on the door and put his face close to the glass. The dog jumped up on the other side, snarling, biting at the window and the man stumbled back from the small stoop, fell into the snow. The door opened and the dog was on him, licking his face.

"Tank! Git off him! Tank, you miserable son of a bitch. I said git off him!"

The voice was gravel and glass. When he looked up he saw Tank sitting at the feet of the old man and the old man scratching the dog behind the ears.

"What you want knocking on my door at this hour?"

"It's only seven o'clock."

"And it's my door. I don't like visitors after dark." The man looked him over. "You're from the ditch I bet, huh?"

"What? I mean, yeah. My car's back about a mile or so."

"I know where it is. More or less." The old man turned and the dog followed him. "Come on inside while I get my boots." He followed the old man in and wiped his shoes on the rug. The warmth of the house had a sweet smell, almost rotten. Tank lay under the small kitchen table. The dog sighed and closed its eyes. In the light, he could see that the dog was very old. Tank licked away snow from his gray muzzle.

The old man came back in wearing a blue stocking cap patched with the logo of a local trucking firm. He wore an old corduroy jacket lined with wool. The old man gestured to one of the four wooden chairs. "Sit," he said. The young man did.

"How did you know I was in the ditch?" he asked.

"Your feet's covered with snow and you're dressed like a moron." The old man almost smiled as he pulled his boots on. They were rubber and closed with metal clasps. "And you ain't the first. Most of the time it's women though."

The old man gave him a khaki parka and rubber boots that slipped on over his shoes, a hat like his own and a pair of thin mittens. He whistled to Tank and the tired mutt dragged itself from under the table. He let the younger man go into the snow first and then followed behind with the dog. The old man started down the drive, toward the road. The snow was still coming down but the wind had died.

"Hey, uh, Sir, where's your truck?"

"Don't have a truck."

"How are you going to pull me out?"

"You ever been in a war?"

"No."

"I have. For a day. I broke my back jumping out of a plane in Korea. They sent me home before I could kill anyone. Why weren't you in Iraq? Or that other one?"

"I don't know. College. Not interested in the military I guess."

The old man stopped. He looked the young man over again while the dog trotted ahead. He started walking again. The young man waited for more, but the old man kept silent except for his breathing.

"I mean it." The young man said. "We're not going to get the car out without a truck. Let's go back. If you'd let me use your phone I can call a tow." The old man shook his head.

"Know what they charge for a tow? Especially in winter when they know they got you by the nuts?"

"No, not off hand."

"Me neither. Cause I never called one." The old man kept walking and the young man followed. Tank held lead, sniffing out their path through the snow.

They passed the spot where the young man was pretty sure the car had gone into the ditch, but there were no tracks so he wasn't certain. They walked on and he made a plan to flag down the first car he saw.

"Roads are dead." The old man said. "Most people got sense it seems."

"Look, I had to work. I was going home. I can't help it if I had to drive."

"You could have helped it going into the ditch, numb nuts. Then I wouldn't be out here freezing my tail off. Tank neither."

"I never asked you to come out here. I just wanted a phone."

"Your parents die young?"

"No. What's that got to do with anything?"

The old man hocked and spit. "It'd be a reason for them not teaching you to show some grace when someone does you a favor." The young man looked further down the road and then behind. There were no headlights.

The dog turned into a hidden drive about another mile down the road. The men followed. There was a small house set back among the trees. A light burned inside. The old man pulled the young man by the sleeve, to a small wooden shed set off to the side. The door was secured with a padlock.

"Kick the door in," the old man said.

"What? No. You kick it in."

"I can't. I'm too old. Do it."

"Hell no. You're crazy."

"You want to get your car out of the ditch? I need you to do me a favor. This is my daughter's place. Go ahead. Kick the door in."

"Isn't your daughter going to be pissed? Busting into her shed?"

"She's dead two years. So no, I don't think she'll mind." The young man looked at the old man. "Quit starin' at me and do it, you dumb son of a bitch."

The young man sighed. He gave the door a few half-hearted kicks. Tank sat in the snow and watched.

"I can't do it."

"You some kind of Mary? Kick it like you'd kick a man's head in! Kick it like you want to kill it."

The young man kicked the door again, harder. He backed up and kicked again. He wanted to kick the old man. The door shook and he kicked again. And again.

The door swung open with a splintering crack and the old man entered the dark shed. The young man looked at the house but aside from the light inside it was dead. The old man rattled around inside the shed, metal clanking and crashing. He came out holding a wood handled hammer. He thrust it into the young man's gut as he passed. "C'mon now," he said. The young man and the dog followed. The old man stepped to the door and pounded hard. The young man joined him, the hammer at his side.

"What are we doing? You said she was dead."

"Her husband's here. He's got a truck that'll do the job."

They waited. "I don't think he's here," the young man said.

"He's here. He's always here."

There were footsteps inside and then a face in the window. The man opened the door and stepped outside. He a smallish man, but wiry, gray and hard-looking, self-made, like experience had given him what breeding couldn't.

"What you want, Marty? Who's your friend?"

"He ain't a friend. I hired him to put the claw end of this hammer through your skull."

The husband laughed. He looked at the young man. "That right, junior? You here to do me in? You listening to Marty's stories and come to dish out some justice?"

And what he meant to do was tell the man he didn't know what the old man was talking about, that he was an old coot and all he'd wanted was to use the phone. But it was so cold. The hammer tapped a quickening beat against his thigh, thumping along with his heart.

Corbin's Dreams Take Flight

Corbin Rutherford Scaggs fell off the roof of the single-wide trailer he shared with his mom and older brother Tommy. His wrist was fixed with five pins and a titanium plate and the surgeon prescribed him Percocet, but it didn't really matter because Tommy took the pills with him when he skipped out, again.

Corbin gave Tommy a month to come back before he moved his brother's belongings out of their bedroom. He tied everything up in three black garbage bags and tucked them under the trailer, moving a broken section of lattice skirting and dragging the bags behind him as he crawled underneath.

* * *

Corbin drew up the blinds and opened the window. He breathed dusty sunlight and pulled the dry flies out of the window track with the finger tips of his healing hand. He threw them out the hole Tommy had knifed through the screen. He climbed up the ladder to the top bunk, Tommy's bed, and stripped the sheets. He looked at the brown stain, dark at its center and fading though a spectrum of tans and yellows as it spread. He fought the mattress with his bad hand and finally got it flipped over. He lay down on the clean side of the bare mattress and stared at the collection of boogers that dotted the ceiling like stars. Corbin made his own constellations: The Scarecrow, The Fist, The Owl.

* * *

Corbin pulled his sheets from the dryer and brought the clean bundle to his nose, smelled for the bold promises of the dryer sheet box.

"Hey Corbin! Come see!" Corbin looked through the window and saw Janie Myers calling, waving him over a few trailers down. She was still holding that beat-up teddy bear, the bear Corbin was fetching for her when he fell off the roof. It was Tommy who'd thrown it up there.

Corbin tossed the clean sheets up top his new bed and went out to meet Janie. The teddy dangled in one hand and a pellet pistol in the other. Next to her stood the Davis brothers, Jessie with a Daisy bb gun and Rusty with a stick. On the ground in front of them was a pigeon without eyes or a beak, bleeding, flapping a good wing and a broken one. Its legs were broken in half.

"This thing won't die!" Jessie said. His mouth hung open after the last word, slacked and then curving into a grin packed with crooked teeth.

"Whose turn?" Rusty asked. He was a small clone of his big brother. Specks of pigeon blood dotted his face.

"Give Corbin a turn," Janie said. "He can kill it." Corbin watched the bird flop and then picked it up, held it firm as the bird pecked blindly at his hands with its gaping mouth hole.

"Kill it! Kill it!" Rusty said. Corbin looked at Janie and then at the boys. He left with the pigeon.

"Asshole!" Jessie yelled and raised his BB gun. He pumped it quickly and shot, barely aiming, missing. He pumped the gun again, but Corbin was inside the trailer before he took the shot. There was a metallic ping as the BB hit the aluminum door and the bird startled, flapped out of Corbin's hands and fell to the floor.

Corbin found the old Ace bandage from under the bathroom sink and wrap up the bird. "This'll keep you still." He said. "Warm too." He left the immobile bird on the small kitchen table and went to the freezer. He pulled a double orange popsicle from the icebox, ripped off the paper and melted the whole thing under the kitchen tap. He found some clear tape in the junk drawer and went back to the bird. He held a popsicle stick to the bird's legs for a quick measurement and put the stick in his mouth. He shook it between his clenched molars until it broke to the proper length.

"I'm sorry. I know it hurts." Corbin straightened the leg and held it firm to the stick. He fumbled with his free, bad hand and pulled the tape from the roll using his teeth again. He dropped the roll and wrapped the tape around the stick and leg until it was a tight splint. He did the same with the other leg.

* * *

Corbin dug with his hands under the trailer. The dirt was cool and damp from the shade and the perpetual slow leak from one of the pipes that ran underneath the trailer. He found a small earthworm, and then another. He put them into a plastic cup as he found more of them. Soon the cup was filled halfway and he crawled back toward the open lattice. Rusty and Jessie squatted at the entrance, watching him. They had their bb gun and stick.

"I want the bird back," Jessie said.

"Well I ain't givin' him to you so you can kill him."

"He's ours," Rusty said. "We found him on our porch."

"He's nobody's," Corbin said. He looked at the BB gun in Jessie's hands. Jessie smiled and raised the gun.

"I pumped it twenty times. It'll break the skin, might even break your jugular."

"Then you'll die!" Rusty said.

"For a bird," Jessie added. "Give him back. He's ours."

Corbin looked at the brothers and thought about Tommy. He wondered if he was ever coming back. Now would be a good time. Tommy would snatch up both of the boys by the scruff and kick their asses all the way back home. But then he'd probably kill the bird himself.

"Alright." Corbin said. "He's inside. Let me out and I'll get him." The boys moved and the light shone in the opening again. Corbin scooted on his butt through the dirt, holding the cup of worms. He stood and replaced the lattice. The brothers walked ahead. Corbin walked up quietly behind, snatched the stick from Rusty and cracked Jessie upside the head. Rusty went for the stick, clawing Corbin's arm. Corbin shot a hard knee into the boy's groin and dropped him to the ground. Jessie was laid out, reaching for the BB gun. Corbin raised the stick cracked him hard across the knuckles over and over until the boy gave up on the rifle. Corbin panted. The Davis boys cried in the dirt.

"Sorry," Corbin said. He stepped over them and went back into the trailer with the worms.

The pigeon had managed to wriggle out of the bandage, and it was lying on the yellow linoleum. Corbin rewrapped the bird and placed it back on the table. He pulled out a plastic cereal bowl from the dish pile in the sink and placed a few worms in it. He added milk. He took a large spoon and worked like an apothecary with a mortar and pestle, grinding the worms and milk into a gray paste. With a tiny measuring spoon Corbin began feeding the bird's open hole. It couldn't swallow and the paste flowed out over the bird and the table.

* * *

Rusty Davis answered the trailer door. Through the outer screen Corbin could see Jessie watching cartoons. Jessie turned around and spoke for Rusty.

"What the hell do you want? You got our bird?"

"I need the beak," Corbin said.

* * *

Corbin again removed the lattice skirt of the trailer and crawled underneath. The Davis boys followed. Corbin untied a bag and began fishing through Tommy's contents: clothes, stiff pornography magazines, action figures, papers and trash. In the second bag, Corbin found a two-piece ceramic ashtray. He removed the lid and peaked inside, handed it to Jessie. Rusty moved in to look. The tray was full of fat marijuana roaches.

"So give me the beak," Corbin said.

"Can we have the pornos?" Rusty asked.

Inside the trailer, Corbin and the brothers looked down on the bird, the mess of worm paste and the bird's own filth smeared on the Formica tabletop.

"You fixed his legs," Rusty said. "Jesus, he's a mess."

"You guys did this." Corbin said.

"Can we smoke this in here?" Jessie asked.

"I guess. My mom isn't coming home till after dark."

"We should get the bird high," Rusty said. Jessie punched him in the arm. "Ow! I'm being for real. Like how doctors give it out in California." He turned to Corbin. "Shouldn't we?"

Corbin thought. "It can't do him any worse." He rolled the upper and lower beak parts between his fingers. "And we need him calm."

The brothers lit a big roach from Tommy's ashtray and took turns at it, holding the smoke in their lungs before blowing it into the bird's eyeless, beakless face. Corbin searched the junk drawer again and found a small tube of super glue.

"That going to work?" Jessie squeaked.

"It's what they used to close up my wrist. Same kind of stuff."

Corbin sat at the table. The bird squirmed in the bandage.

"Hold him still, huh?"

Jessie put his hands around the bird. "It's all right," He told the pigeon. Corbin applied the glue in a thin strip around the edge of the beak. He held it tight against the bird.

"The tube says thirty seconds," Rusty said. The boys held silent for over a minute. Corbin pulled his hands away slowly and the beak looked good, it held. The boys smiled. Corbin went to work on the top half of the beak, rolled it into position between his fingers and applied another thin strip of glue.

"I think you need some more," Rusty said over Corbin's shoulder.

"Shut up." Jessie said. "He knows what he's doing."

"Both of you be quiet. Hold him still." Corbin pressed the beak to the hole and held it tight. It looked perfect. It was the best anyone could have done.

He pulled his hand away. The bird followed. "Oh shit. I glued it to my fingers."

* * *

Corbin lay in his bed staring up at the bottom of Tommy's old mattress between the support rungs. The graduated staining reminded him of a chopped tree and he counted the rings. He wondered if he should trade mattresses. The pigeon lay on his chest, still except for the up and down movement of Corbin's breathing. Corbin looked into the dry eye sockets and wondered what birds saw in the dark of their own heads.

"You're going to be okay," he said as he stroked the bird's neck. Corbin pulled tentatively, but his fingers held firm to the beak and the beak held firm to the bird. Corbin closed his eyes and tried to be a bird.

Jessie and Rusty said their dad had a gas can in the back of his truck they could get. That was a while ago. Corbin hoped the gas would work. He was thinking maybe a razor blade was a good idea when the brothers finally came back, pounding on the trailer door.

"Corbin!" Jessie yelled. "Corbin! We got the gas!"

Corbin opened the door and the sun shone in warm and bright. He squinted. He didn't see Janie there behind Rusty until he stepped outside. She was holding the red gas can.

"Dad's can was empty." Jessie said. "We had to walk down to the Shell. Janie paid for it."

Corbin looked at the girl. She tucked her greasy hair behind her ear with her fingers.

"Was just a dollar," she said, looking at her shoes.

She was held the bear under her arm and Corbin wondered when the pair of them had last been washed. And then he looked at the girl and realized she was very pretty, a grubby little beauty with head lice. Janie noticed him looking at her and she blushed. She kicked at the ground in her beat up, oversized All-Stars and waved the gas can back and forth. The solvent sloshed around inside.

Jessie had Corbin sit on the ground with his arm out. Rusty held the bird still while Jessie pulled the plastic cap from the nozzle. Jessie brought it to his nose and inhaled deep and long.

"Ever huff this stuff?" He asked. He sat Indian style where boy met bird and doused the connection with gasoline. "All right, try to work your fingers free."

Corbin pulled, but his fingers weren't separating from the beak. "Pour a little more," He said.

There was a shriek and Corbin recognized it as the loose timing belt on his mom's old Cutlass. He looked down the main drag of the trailer park and saw the two-toned beast turning into the lot.

"Oh shit! Hurry up! Man, my mom's going to kick my ass when she sees the mess on the table."

"I'm trying man, pull!" Jessie poured more gasoline and doused the bird.

"Ah hell!" Corbin said.

"Sorry! Sorry!"

The car stopped with a squeak of the brakes. Mom was smiling. She held a red and white bucket of chicken under each arm.

"Look who I found!" She said. It was Tommy. Shirtless and hair cut short, shaved to the skin nearly. He had fresh ink on his chest, a cross, and it looked infected. He smiled at Corbin, sucked hard on his cigarette.

"First one of these I had in thirty days! Fucking DOC assholes. Next time I'm goin' on the run. How you doing, shit head?"

Tommy didn't wait for an answer, didn't seem to notice his little brother was glued to a bird. He stomped up the wooden porch and entered the trailer. Mom watched after him, smiling, proud.

"I'm so glad he's home." She turned to Corbin. "You finish up with your friends here and come in to eat with the family." She went inside and the kids just looked at each other, waited.

"Corbin!" Mom yelled. She was outside so fast the word was still in her mouth. "What the hell did you do in here?"

Before Corbin could say anything the trailer door flew open again and Tommy came out, the last quarter of the cigarette clenched between his teeth.

"Asshole! What'd you do with all my shit?!" Tommy pulled the cigarette from his mouth and flicked it at Corbin. The fumes caught fire before the cigarette even hit his hand.

Corbin ran down the length of the park, hand and bird blazing, the unraveling bandage trailing and burning behind him. Jessie finally caught him and tackled him to the ground. Rusty helped hold him down while Janie beat the flames with a stick. Corbin watched her. She was scared, so pretty and scared. She raised the stick again and again, trying to kill the hungry fire. Corbin watched it all in the glossy black eyes of the bear as it stared back, limp at Janie's feet.

You Just Never Know Where It's Been

She looked like the kind of girl who needed to be smacked around a little before the fucking started. She should have said something before.

I got taken in and it was the first time I'd been arrested, but I played it like it wasn't. I was wondering about jailhouse rape and all of that. I crossed paths with a guy once who was a prison guard and of course that's what I asked him about. And he said that there was enough consensual shit going on that no one really got raped too much. Not too much. I figured if I got raped I'd chalk it up to a life experience only a few people get to partake in.

It was mostly just a bunch of drunks drying out and this kid with a poorly fixed harelip who snuck in a joint up his ass. I let the rest of the guys hit it first so I knew they weren't just fucking with me. I tasted ass but the weed was pretty good and the harelip kid told us that they hauled him in for stealing a set of stereo speakers from the place he worked. He said the cops got him by matching up the tire tracks and I thought about that and asked him if he confessed after they told him about the tracks. He said yeah and then I asked him if he worked there long, and if they actually did take the time make casts of his tracks over some speakers, wouldn't it make sense for his tracks to be there? He thought about that for a minute and then hit me in the mouth. Ignorance isn't so much bliss as it's the truth that hurts, dig?

I didn't have anyone to call but the girl who put me in there and I sweet talked her on the phone and she came around and said she'd get me out and that if I was good to her she'd drop the charges. I said I didn't think she could since it wasn't a civil thing but criminal and she started to cry and asked if I'd be nice anyway. I fingered the number of this girl Allie someone had scrawled on the wall over the telephone and said I would if she'd just post bail. I hung up and asked one of the cops if I could make another call.

Allie wasn't home but I talked to her dad and he thanked me for at least not calling collect, but he'd appreciate it if I didn't call again. Allie was after all only fourteen. I said ok but I made sure to commit the number to memory because fourteen or not, a girl doesn't end up on the wall at the county lockup if she isn't good to go.

I slept for a little while and when I woke up the harelip kid was standing over me and his cock was out and I figured here it was and I wondered if I could fight him off and if I wanted to since I was looking for experience, but then he started pissing on me and I grabbed his cock hard in my fist and he sprayed sideways and squealed. I pulled his handle and dragged him to the other side of the holding cell and he started to get hard in my hand. We looked into each others' eyes and his baby blues could have belonged to my mother they were so deep. I didn't know my mother so it was altogether possible I was holding the erect penis of a long lost brother and I imagined me and the kid together, sharing a room as boys, sneaking up and down bunks to fool around and promise never to tell anyone. And then the both of us grown up, families and all that on the holidays, both wondering if the other was thinking that the real party would be happening in the bathroom down the hall. We'd flush the toilet over and over to cover the sounds and everybody would know we were up to some brotherly nonsense, but not that I was letting him piss in my mouth while we jacked each other off.

The guard who let me call Allie called my name and I was sprung and I told the kid, "In another life partner." He smiled and I marveled at how deeply inside myself I had to fall to make a connection with someone.

She drove and asked if I was hungry and I told her yeah so we stopped at a drive-thru and she put her hand on my knee and said she was sorry for the trouble and she wasn't hurt, she was just scared because no one had ever tried to fuck her like that. I said not to worry about it. She asked how it was inside and I told her I slept most the time and didn't really experience any of it. I told her about the joint though and where it came from and she thought it was gross and said she couldn't believe I kissed her after putting something like that in my mouth. She threw the bag of food in my lap and stepped on the gas and she wouldn't shut up and now she was taking the tone of the girl I'd smacked, the one who called the police and started the whole thing. I tuned her out and thought about Allie, the fourteen-year-old jailhouse whore. I wondered when I'd finally get in touch with her and if she would ever cause me this kind of hassle. And I wondered how much of a fight Daddy would put up and if what she wanted was a new one.

A Glass of Water

I sat down at the counter. It was going on midnight and I didn't have a dime.

"Can I have a glass of water, please?"

"Are you going to buy something?" she asked. She was worn and tired. Her plastic nametag had been sprayed with a cream sauce, maybe soup; it said: Kate. Her eyes, cold, said she'd seen me a million times before. Or others like me.

"I don't have any money."

She nodded, bit the left side of her thin bottom lip. "No water, unless you buy something."

"Please? I've been walking a long time."

"Mister, if you don't have any money you got to go. This ain't a well." She wiped her hands on the blue apron, drawing attention to it, reaffirming her station, her authority. The customer was right as long as they could pay the tab.

"Could I use the restroom?" I was sure there was a sink. If not I'd drink from the toilet.

"You going to buy something?" I shook my head and she left me there. I watched the stainless steel doors to the kitchen flap behind her. I listened to the sizzle and steam of the kitchen escape in short bursts as the doors settled back home. Was she getting me the water? I looked around the restaurant. It was empty except for a trio of high school kids smoking cigarettes in a corner booth. They laughed and coughed and blew smoke rings. They'd made a mess of the table with their ashes and food and drinks. The boy with the acne shredded a white napkin for fun. I watched him watch the girl and boy necking across the table. His mouth twitched between drags from his cigarette. The girl squealed and tilted her head back showing her long smooth neck. The napkin-shredder looked away and I heard his boot thumping on the floor. He turned to me and I looked down at the counter, made busy wiping dust away. The motion released a fine misty layer from my jacket.

"How you doing partner?" the bald man burst through the swinging doors, the waitress in tow. He had the face of a lizard, some sort of scaly skin condition affecting his scalp. His eyes were bulbous behind his glasses. He wore the short sleeve oxford and clip on tie of a diner manager. He looked as hard and square as a brick. The waitress remained behind him, looking over his shoulder, a full head taller.

"I'm real thirsty," I said.

"Mm. Well Mister, our policy is that we only serve water to paying customers."

"I told him," the waitress added over his shoulder. The man went on talking, but I was too parched to listen. He said something about loitering and explained the concept of a business to me.

"Can I just sit for a minute then?"

"No," he said. "Not unless you buy something. Don't make me call the sheriff."

"I wouldn't do that." I realized after saying it that the statement sounded like a warning. I wondered if they took my meaning: that I didn't want trouble. I stayed silent and still except for my tongue, which I ran over the dry grooves and bumps of my hard pallet. I imagined cool water, ice clinking in a sweating glass, so cold it burns. I let myself stand on the lip of the glass and fall inside, naked, drinking my fill, the ice sticking to my skin as it rinsed away the grime.

The manager and the waitress stared, waiting for me to turn, to retreat. I looked at the counter again. I poked at a nick, a cutlery slip. I traced the graffiti (Mike was a faggot, JC and Connie were in love). I heard steps behind me, the door opened, jingling a bell.

"Bye now," the waitress said, sweet as the day old pie in the glass case behind her.

"Bye Katy," the girl from the booth said. Her voice drew my eyes up. I saw her reflection in the bakery case. Her dress was white and dotted with yellow threaded flowers, handmade and summery. I saw her boyfriend, tall and hard and smooth skinned, his hand on her sun-browned shoulder. The girl's smile had too many teeth. She looked less beautiful than she had across the restaurant. I bet she was used to compliments, took them as gospel. She didn't realize the size of the pond she was in. I hoped she'd never leave the town.

"He's got it," the guy said thumbing toward the napkin shredder, still in the booth, still shredding.

"Course, he does," the waitress said with a knowing smile.

"Say hi to your daddy for me," the manager said. "Tell him I'm going to take that sow prize this year." I felt like a stranger at a party where everyone knew each other.

"I'll tell him," the guy said, "but I hope you got something special 'cause his is a real beauty."

"How many pounds is she?"

"Hank, I ain't tellin' you shit!" The voice sounded bitter and menacing, but the manager's big eyes glazed with swelling laughter.

"Alright then, alright then." The manager was still laughing after the door swung home and the bell died. He looked at me and for a moment I thought maybe he'd changed his mind, but his humor had followed the couple out the door.

"Didn't I tell you to leave?"

"I told him," the waitress said.

"Please, just a glass of water," I said. "Let me drink from your hose even."

The manager shook his head. "We don't have a hose." He went back through the swinging doors to make good on his word and call the law.

"You shoulda gone when I said so," the waitress said over her shoulder, following.

I looked back at the table, at the boy. The pile of white paper in front of him had grown. He stared at the empty space left by the girl's neck. He lit a cigarette while his previous butt smoldered in the ashtray. He leaned forward on his elbows, blew a tight dark stream of smoke across the table.

The manager and waitress came back. Both of their faces were set in the same smile, victorious.

"Now, you done it," the waitress said.

"I called the sheriff. He's on his way." I focused on the calloused tip of the stubby finger he pointed at me. "You best git."

I nodded, rubbed my hands together. I looked straight up, head back, and let the cool breeze from the duct above me hit my face and neck.

"Just give him a god damned glass of water." The napkin shredder stared into his white pile. He had no more napkins. He was out of fuel.

"Manny," the manager said. "Don't you start." Manny didn't look at him, just kept on looking into the pile of white. "The man is thirsty. Give him a drink of water and he'll go."

The manager looked at me and I nodded, as slight and humble as I could, but the prospect of that cool drink shook me hard.

"Water's for paying customers. No water unless you buy somethin'."

To Bananas

He wanted the banana the way he wanted the girl, but the girl wasn't an option. The fruit was still green and firm, large and heavy in his hand, weapon like.

"Just the banana."

"Thirty cents," the small Mexican said.

He paid with two quarters and dropped the two dimes into the coffee can next to the register. He didn't know what the money went to: cancer, spastic kids, a local family who couldn't afford a funeral. It was in Spanish and he didn't speak it. He left the store, the banana still heavy and dangerous in his hand. He put it in the pocket of his old pea coat for later. He had the banana and now he didn't want it. What he wanted was to be out of the desert. It was his first night in Tucson and so far he hated it. He didn't start teaching for four months, but his friends had asked him out early to house sit when they left for the summer. His skin was salty from moving his belongings into his weekly-rate, one-room rental with the broken shower. His friends had said the heat could be oppressive, but the night had cooled and he was walking comfortably, glad for the coat. He should have bought them a gift. Wine was traditional, but they were meeting at a bar. There was nothing they needed. No one *needed* anything. If you knew that, you had something.

His boots landed heavy on each wooden stair as he entered the narrow passage leading up to their favorite spot, The Ship. The décor was minimal; several fishing nets were strung from the ceiling, a ship in a bottle was mounted over the bar next to an old brass telescope. The atmosphere was in truth due to the shape of the establishment, concaved, wood planked walls that widened the room as they reached for the ceiling.

He saw her first, her stone cut features strong, but feminine, smooth. Her hair was pulled back in a ponytail and she reminded him of the girl from college he knew before she married. She was talking loudly, but he couldn't make out the words over the noise of the other patrons. The Ship was an academic hideaway, two blocks from the university, yet free of drunken undergrads. Most of the conversation was professional or theoretical or philosophical; grants and publications took the place of children. Dark corners held small tables lit by candles for associate professors and their current graduate assistants.

Paul saw him first and stood up to meet him, greeted him with a smile and a sigh.

"Thank God you're here. If I had to hear anymore about- what the hell are you talking about?"

She smiled at him and then rolled her eyes toward Paul. She stood and kissed his cheek. "We were having a discussion about dreams. What do you think? Do dreams mean anything beyond the literal or do they represent some unconscious phenomena?"

"Yeah," Paul said, "is this a cigar in my hand? Or something else?"

She shook her head and rolled her eyes again. "Oh shut up. I'm not talking some Freudian repression phallus cliché. I'm talking about the mystical, the unseen world beyond," she waved a hand over all she saw, "this. Is a dream just my brain sorting through all the garbage or is there something more to it?"

Paul laughed at her. "I already know what he's going to say. He's going to say that without data, it's worthless."

"Why don't you let him answer, Paul?" she said. Paul scoffed and held up his beer toward his friend, conceding the floor.

"Without data it's worthless." He said. He believed it too- despite intentionally arousing the laughter of Paul and a few peripheral eggheads listening nearby- he truly did. To him, ideas from nowhere were nowhere ideas. She gave him that hurt, angry look he knew so well, the fake one she gave only to him, the same one she gave when he was her tough love chemistry tutor in college.

"See?" Paul said. "What did I tell you? Where's the waitress?"

"However," he continued, overtaking Paul. "That doesn't mean there's nothing to it. We shouldn't make that mistake. Absence of evidence isn't evidence of absence."

She smiled at Paul, vindicated, but Paul was still looking for the waitress. Their friend continued, "But then, if that's the logic we go with, who's to say dreams aren't aliens messing with our heads at night, replacing the memories of kidnapping and probing with our own surreal television programming?"

"So you're saying all points of view are equally valid?" She asked him.

"Not at all. I'd say all points of view are equally *invalid*. Until we have evidence that is."

Paul emptied his beer mug and stood. "I don't think she's coming back. I'm going to get another round. Ready?" The pair nodded. She watched Paul leave and leaned across the table, toward him.

"Give me one of those?" she said pointing to the pack of cigarettes sticking out of his shirt pocket. He knew she didn't have a light so he struck a match for her and she leaned in closer, sucking the flame into the end of the tobacco tube, taking a long first drag. He watched her eyes watch for Paul to return. She leaned back and blew the smoke above her, showing her sun browned neck.

"It's a small betrayal," she said. "But I allow myself one whenever I can get away with it."

"I know," he said. "This isn't the first time you've asked me to conspire."

She smiled and grabbed his hand across the table. "I'm so glad you're out here. God, we missed you. I hate it when people drift out of our lives and you never know if they'll drift back in. You know what I mean?"

"How are you guys?"

"He's busy. We'll be back in Ghana all summer. *Supposed* to be. I'm thinking about staying back here. He doesn't know that though, so keep quiet. Did you know I got malaria last year?"

"You told me. It was in the holiday card."

"Of course," She said. She looked up and past him before taking another long drag and then crushing the cherry into the clean ashtray. "If I have to eat one more plantain or bowl of fufu." She smelled her fingers and pulled a small plastic bottle of hand sanitizer from her bag. It smelled of alcohol and aloe.

"Don't start," she said. "I know I'm doing the world a disservice."

"We need germs," he said.

"Oh, I'm aware of your stance on germs. Is your apartment a pit of filth yet?"

"Apartment? There's a stretch. As for its state, I'd call it an experiment. 'Pit of filth' is kind of a harsh judgment."

"This goes against every feminist instinct in me, but if there was ever anyone who needed a woman around, it's you."

"Now *that* is a harsh judgment."

She laughed. "You're exactly the same as in college. You know that?"

"Unfortunately, yes."

Paul came back holding two beer mugs by the handles and two gin and tonics cupped in his other hand. "Still drinking these, I assume?"

"You know he is. I was just telling him how he hasn't changed a bit. Drink, drink. You need to catch up with us."

He took a series of long swallows, savoring the bitter fizz and lime until the ice cubes clinked against his teeth. He put the empty glass on the table and sipped from the second. The alcohol warmed him quickly. He reached into his pocket.

"I picked up something for you two. It isn't a plantain, but it's close." He laid the green banana on the table.

"That's the biggest damn banana I've ever seen," Paul said. "You could beat someone with that thing."

"Maybe," he said. He pulled out a cigarette, absently offered one to her. She shook her head. "When do you two leave for Ghana anyway? You're both going, no?"

He looked at her and again she gave him the look, but this time the eyes may have meant it. She leaned forward before Paul could answer the question. She raised her mug. "To bananas," she said.

The three glasses clinked, and just for a moment the edges formed a perfect triangle that no one but the waitress could see as she came up from behind, her hair a frizzy mess on top of her head, her apron strings loose and flowing.

I Love the Devil

My dad moved us out of the city and bought The Diablo bar and restaurant with the insurance money after mom got burned alive. We all got burned but Mom was the only one who died. I was just a baby and my scars are the worst since kids heal so fast. It's mostly my legs, they're shiny and hairless. Dad's scars are just on half of him and they make him look older than his thirty-nine years, his left side anyway. Dad says scars give you character, a story to tell. I don't show my scars ever, not even when it gets real humid during the monsoon. I wear long pants year round.

The Diablo isn't a restaurant anymore, just a bar. We serve pretzels and peanuts and have a free taco bar on Tuesdays and it's my job to sweep up the crumbs and pieces of shell at the end of the night. I'm too young to be in there the hours that I am but no one minds, not even the cops or border patrol who come in after their shifts, they just know I'm Ernie's kid and that's that. They used to scruff my hair when I was younger, shorter, just a kid. Now they just give me a nod or raise their beer to me or say "hello." One cop, Deputy Lou used to scruff my hair so hard I thought he'd rub my head as bald as my legs. He stopped when the rest of them did though and I liked him the best of all because he let me play with his hand cuffs.

Lou even let me shoot his gun behind The Diablo one night. We got a bunch of empty liquor bottles from the trash and set them up in a row on the old fence that separates our property from the Yaqui reservation. Lou said I was a good shot even though I only hit about half of the bottles. He cleaned up the rest of them without even aiming.

He got shot near the border last year and died. He was crooked they said, dealing with the cartels and smuggling in Horse and Glass, that's what they call it, the heroin and meth.

Maria is the bartender. The first time she came in she was bleeding and crying, really hysterical like my mom screamed in my nightmares and I had to wonder if she was on fire. Everyone in the place just watched her, kind of dumbstruck, except for Dad. He came from behind the bar and she grabbed him like she was drowning and he was a piece of driftwood. We didn't even know if she spoke English because she just kept saying "mi Hermano, mi Hermano" which is "my brother" in Spanish. The brother she cried for had been shot at the gas station down the street by her boyfriend. The boyfriend came in holding a big revolver. He was a big Mexican and looked mean, sweaty and dirty and hard as rock with no shirt. I was really scared, but Dad wasn't. He just said "Calm down hombre, easy now." The boyfriend saw Maria in Dad's arms and pointed the gun at them and pulled the trigger but he was out of bullets. Deputy Lou was there and put two bullets into the boyfriend's stomach. And that was it. Maria came in everyday to work after that. She felt she owed Dad her life and Dad finally just gave her a job. Maria's got a beautiful voice and every night she sings old Mexican folk songs and dances while my father plays along on acoustic guitar. Nobody can order drinks while she sings, but they never complain. My favorite song is this one about the mountains and how when they're covered with snow they're about as pretty as a woman, naked and waiting. I had to write down the lyrics like I heard them and took them to the library to translate but couldn't find the words in the Spanish dictionary since they were spelled wrong. I asked an old Mexican at The Diablo that night what they meant and he wrote them on a napkin with red ink and I snuck him a free bourbon, then I watched Maria sing while Dad played and when she smiled at me I fell in love with her.

That same night after closing, I was sweeping and Dad played guitar and I asked Maria if she would marry me one day when I was old enough. She took my chin in her hand and kissed me on the mouth and I tasted the dust on her lips and she told me she wished she was young again. Dad just watched her and smiled and kept playing with his old burned side turned away from us.

That Boy Got Dynamite in His Hands

We heard Harold's dad crying through the door of his bedroom and I wondered how long it had been going on, how long he'd been locked in his bedroom while Harold and I lit off M-80s in the backyard, the real ones, military grade. I imagined the grown man jumping with each gunpowder explosion, with each voiceover scream Harold and I play acted to convince ourselves we knew death. The sound from the bedroom made me wish I was among the scorched red shells of the tiny bombs, blown to pieces and shaking in the wind, dancing over the melted and limbless plastic army men, men left to the wild things that pick battlefields clean.

The noise behind the door sounded just like Harold whenever he used to cry on the playground, like when that big bastard Bryan Babin pushed him off the monkey bars and Harold landed hard on his tailbone and had to sit on one of those old people toilet pads for almost a month. It sounded just like that, except his dad had a man's voice while Harold's was that of a kid with an old man's name. I'd heard my own dad cry, but it didn't sound the same. Dad sounded like the movies and he only did it when he used to beg my mom not to go. The sound from Harold's dad was a soul stripped of its skin.

Harold made us bologna sandwiches with mustard and we listened to the chewing sounds in our ears instead of the crying. When it finally stopped we didn't have to pretend anymore, but it was too quiet so we watched an old Western movie on Harold's big screen and turned the surround sound way up.

"What?" Harold asked me. The sound of the gunfire followed the action left to right and then behind us as the poncho-clad hero slapped at the hammer of his revolver with an open palm six times, the reports calling for blood. A body fell and flailed from its perch atop the saloon, and the old cowboy's death bellow shook the house, rattled our crumb covered plates in the sink.

"'Does your dad ever hit you?' I said."

"No. Does yours?"

"No."

The families' dream house had two staircases leading to the second floor, one on each end, and when we finally went up to Harold's bedroom we used the one farthest away from his dad's room. We played video games for a while, this motorcycle game where you were in this road race and had to beat the other riders with pipes and stuff and then there's bikini girls waiting at the end, all smiles and boobs. After I died I lay down on Harold's bed and looked at the ceiling while he played. The ceiling was so smooth, new, not like the flaking popcorn ceiling in my basement room with the big yellow spot from when my dad overfilled the waterbed upstairs. My face flushed when I remembered the stain; I always thought that if people from school saw it they'd accuse me of pissing on the ceiling. It was a ridiculous fear- but maybe not.

One time after Harold wouldn't give Bryan Babin his basketball at school, Bryan started saying that Harold ate shit and everyone believed it, or at least they agreed for the sake of ridicule. They all screamed together in a big circle around him on the basketball court at middle recess, "Shit Eater, Shit Eater!" I knew he didn't eat shit, but I was with them, hiding in the back, saying the words to preserve the last of what I mistook for dignity. If Harold saw me, he never said anything.

Harold was one of the cool kids until Bryan started picking on him, and then he was friends with me. By fifth grade, we allowed ourselves a bit of optimism since Bryan was a year older and it was only one more year until he was on to the junior high and out of our lives. When we came back to school the next fall we found Bryan was held back a year and in our class. Nothing changed. Harold was still Shit Eater. Together we were a couple of "homos."

Harold's dad looked in on us, his lanky arms dangling from lanky fingertips hooked atop the doorframe molding. He gave his son a smile, nodded to me, still smiling but dropping the tenderness like something too heavy to carry. His eyes didn't look red or puffy or anything, and I thought that he looked really handsome, like a celebrity even, which was funny because the man had a big handlebar moustache with the ends curled with wax. It should have made him look older or at least old-fashioned, but on him it looked odd and interesting, like an old-timey boxer back when they called it fisticuffs and the guys fought bare-knuckle fights lasting over a hundred rounds. I only knew about fisticuffs from a song I listened to on one of my dad's old cassette tapes and every time I heard the song I saw Harold's dad in the ring, battling some unyielding opponent round after round, a battle not of skill, not of strength, but of wills.

Harold's dad watched us for a long time and his presence made me uneasy. I was afraid he'd start crying again, but I couldn't look away from him despite that fear. I watched the man as he watched his son's progress through the race, the violent braining of competition. I watched and waited for the man to blink but he never did, and to me it was like he kept wide-eyed because he was afraid he'd miss something important, like the opposite of clenching your eyes shut when you're scared of what you'll see. Harold finally finished and looked up from the screen. I looked away from his dad. I blinked.

"Hi pop."

"You guys want some lunch? I made potato soup."

"We had bologna," Harold said. His dad looked at me for an answer and even though Harold's dad was an amazing cook and I drooled at the thought of covering the thick, creamy soup with shredded cheddar cheese and bacon and green onion, the image of me eating soup with just Harold's dad made me feel weird, like we were nothing more than surrogates for something else. Or more that *he* was a surrogate and I was just a kid eating his soup.

"I had bologna too," I said. Harold's dad nodded and left us alone. I wanted to call after him, ask him why he'd been crying, have him pull me to him and tell me it was okay. I asked the question in my mind and the scene that played out was so vivid I had to shake myself free, like when I replayed uncomfortable home movies in my mind. I was still vibrating when Harold finally spoke.

"What's with you?"

"Nothing."

"Let's go outside."

We were walking down the driveway when Harold's mom pulled up in the station wagon. She was pretty, not like touch yourself pretty, but comforting, nice pretty, probably because she was always smiling. She always seemed so happy, but given the little I knew about Harold's family I didn't know how she managed to do it, to stay happy. Harold's dad had worked from home but something happened. He'd lost interest, something she'd called his "funk." Now she had two jobs and was just home for a few hours before going out again.

Harold had told me that the funks came and went as long as he could remember, and that sometimes his dad needed a little time to "get it together." The current funk had been going on for a while. I thought about the words my dad had said when I did my best to confide in him about it. Maybe I wanted assurance that it wouldn't happen to him, maybe I just wanted to know more and hoped Dad's age would give him some kind of insight I was missing. Wasn't the fear of life supposed to end once we grow up?

"He needs to suck it up," he'd said. "Self-pity is a luxury some of us can't afford. But I guess when you're them." That was all he said and I hated him for it. "Them," like Harold's family was something different, something other than we were, different and not deserving of my concern. They were different, but I'd always seen them as something to hold up, to aspire to, the "dream home" as they called it, built upon the work of Harold's dad, at least they had a dream. And their house was a welcoming place full of something other than the fear I knew. I watched Dad as he watched the TV and then I went back to Harold's, hating myself for not saying something to the man. I replayed the scene but none of the retorts were right. What I could have said, I didn't know, but I'm pretty sure that was the day Dad overflowed the waterbed and that act seemed to sum up my feelings for me.

"Hi guys!" Harold's mom said. "Where you off to?"

"Just walking," Harold said.

"Behave, no smoking!" she said. I didn't know how she knew, but then she started laughing and I knew she was kidding. She must have read my eyes though because she kind of cocked her head and arched an eyebrow.

"We're *haive*, Mom, relax. Dad made potato soup."

"Oh yeah?" She brightened and it was almost blinding. "Must be a good day."

I gave Harold a look, but he didn't share it. He shrugged. "I guess." And I followed him down the driveway. When I looked back, his mom was stuffing new information flyers into the plastic box affixed to the realty sign stabbed into their browning lawn. I couldn't see if she was smiling or not, but I told myself she was.

We stomped through the woods, exerting our power over the rustling death and decay with my dad's cigarettes hanging from our lips. We rolled big logs to look for salamanders, each of us on an end, grunting and blowing smoke from dragon noses. We saw no salamanders and I hoped it was just too cold for them and they were wintering in the soil. The summer before, right before junior high started, we found about two hundred of them in an hour, put them all in a big bucket and showed Harold's dad. We'd planned to take them back to the woods but we forgot, and by the time we remembered the whole bucket full had dried out in the sun, stiffening red salamanders all stuck together in a dead and dying mass. Maybe that's why there were no more.

"See any?" Harold said through clenched lips and teeth.

"Nuh uh."

"Think we killed them all?" he asked.

"I was thinking that. It was an accident."

"My dad says there aren't accidents, just stupidity."

"Think we're stupid?"

"My dad said we were, that day anyway."

"You told him?"

"Yeah. I felt bad. He was pretty mad. Said what if someone came along and plucked him up and killed him, or my mom. Would I call it an accident?"

"Would you?"

"'Lack of foresight,' he called it."

I wondered if Harold's dad knew we just threw them in the garbage can, and the idea that he did made my face hot. When my own dad was mad I got scared, but I never felt guilty. I'd take fear over guilt any day; I knew this feeling was going to be with me for a long time, another scene to shake away. My fears always seemed to recede quickly, while shame and embarrassment lingered, my mind playing the scenes over and over in an act of penance that never relieved anything.

"Want to go over to the grade school?" Harold asked.

"Yeah, sure." And we went on, not bothering to turn any more logs.

The edge of the forest opened up to this arboretum with a suspension bridge that hanged over Rush Creek by the high school, right next door to our old elementary school. Before junior high, a lot of recesses were spent eyeballing the parking lot, full of the big kids. They looked so old- girls with boobs and boys with cars, all with freedom. They could leave at lunch time and go to McDonald's or JJ's Pizza if they wanted. Such realizations made the green hot dogs they fed us in the cafeteria hop around in our guts in protest.

There used to be a gazebo in the arboretum but somebody blew it up with a pipe bomb. They caught who did it, this high schooler who was the older brother of this kid a couple years behind us. He was on the news getting arrested and everything, and I watched the TV and saw him cover his face with his jacket like a real criminal. The on-scene footage showed all this wooden debris and a big burnt patch of ground where it had happened, but now as we entered the area from the bridge, the grass was extra thick and dark green where the gazebo had been, from the fertilizer in the bomb I guess.

There was a shallow pond on the old school yard that froze over in winter and some of the kids ice-skated or played hockey on it. Harold and I never did, not even when we went to school there, but now we liked to visit the pond when there was no school and smoke cigarettes and just sit and pretend to fish with broken and bark-stripped switches. Sometimes we brought juice in a thermos and passed it back and forth pretending it was beer, and then later we'd stumble home and play drunken old men.

As soon as the pond came into view I wanted to turn around and run. Bryan Babin was there with a metal hoe and he was slapping at the surface of the water with it. Harold and I watched him from the tree line. We were exposed but I took comfort in reaching my hand behind us to feel the botanic veil of safety. We watched Bryan stalk around the pond, bent over looking for something. Every few steps he'd stop and raise the hoe above his head like a lumberjack over a log or a gladiator slave preparing to kill another, and he'd bring it down with a splash at the water's edge. I took a breath to make the words, "let's go," but Harold started walking toward the pond and Bryan. I hesitated and then followed just behind.

"Gimme a cigarette," Harold said. He took two from the pack, lit them in unison and gave me back the pack and one of the smokes. Bryan looked up as we approached, startled briefly before letting his face take on the mask of contempt we knew well.

"I was wondering when a couple of homos were gonna show up," he said. "What are the fags doing?"

Harold took a drag from the cigarette. "I don't know," he said. "What *are* you doing?" Harold's balls, the break from his usual, subordinate character made my stomach drop, made the hairs stand up all over my body and I felt like I was floating, not only watching Harold, but watching myself too. It was a psychic separation, my mind knowing I should leave but my body was unable, unwilling.

"You want to die, Shit Eater?" Bryan said. He looked at me as if to access my complicacy, to wrangle me further in with some personal insult, but I closed my eyes and he dismissed me, put his attention back on Harold. He lifted the hoe to his shoulder. "I'm killing frogs. I'll kill a couple big faggy ones too." And we saw the pile, or I saw it. I felt that Harold had known all along what Bryan was doing. I stared at the pile of green death for a long time, there must have been at least thirty frogs, mutilated, spilling their guts and drying out in the last of the summer sun. The flies were buzzing, lighting upon the bounty and flying off again when their tiny hairs were touched by threat of a stray breeze. I felt that breeze and again wanted to retreat back to the woods, away from there, back to my room and the piss-stained ceiling. Harold put the cigarette to his lips and watched Bryan watch us. "Say something, faggot. Give me a reason."

"Why'd you do that?" Harold said looking at the pile of frogs.

Bryan laughed. "Felt like it." And as if he sensed what would hurt us even more than words or a beating, he began his hunt again, stalking the perimeter of the pond.

"Stop it," Harold said. Bryan ignored him. He lifted the hoe and brought it down hard before using it to scoop up another dead frog and fling it to the pile. "I said, 'stop'!"

"You gonna tell on me? Go ahead, I'll tell on you for smoking. You know your mommies will cry if I do. Yours anyway, Shit Eater." Harold looked at me, and I didn't like it, his eyes trying to detect my hurt. I didn't like it because it felt like it came from a place of curiosity, not concern, a prodding of depths I'd insisted were dark and barren, a place without life-sustaining light. Harold turned back to Bryan who began stalking again, lifting the hoe and smashing the frogs, their eyes poking out above the brown meniscus, betraying them. I wanted to get out of there, let it go, and as Harold stepped forward I grabbed his arm and he shook my hand loose. He stepped to the edge of the pond, Bryan directly across from him on the other side. Bryan continued his assault, looking up with his gap toothed grin and sad eyes, gauging our pain and frustration. Harold reached into his pocket and pulled out an M-80. He put the cherry of his cigarette to the green wick and it began to hiss.

"Bryan, catch!" he said and he tossed the tiny bomb over the water. Bryan looked up, puzzled by the flying object, and with reflex more than thought, his hand came up to snatch it out of the air. The tiny bomb exploded before he even realized what he held. I watched Harold start to smile as the hoe fell from Bryan's grip, disappeared into the clouded pond. My ears rang out and Bryan began to scream. It was a grotesque sound, the girlish squeal coming from this one dimensional boy I'd known for so long, someone I thought capable of only inflicting pain, not feeling it. Bryan looked at his hand, then to smiling Harold, and back to his hand. His face was whiter than his white-blond hair. Blood dripped steadily from the place where his ring and pinky fingers were previously attached to his hand. The middle finger dangled, connected by a tiny flap of skin. The breeze picked up and the force was enough to complete the separation as I watched that third finger fall away into the muddy water.

I couldn't move and probably would have stood there all night if Harold hadn't pulled me away. I chased after him into the woods, ran hard through the branches, the thorny claws grabbing and scratching, ripping my clothes and slicing my sweaty face. Bryan's screams followed behind much longer than they should have been able, jabbing at me like the tiny thistles tagging along on my clothes. I kept Harold in my sight, saw nothing *but* Harold.

We were exhausted by the time we exited the woods. Our young bodies were defying us and neither one could run any farther. We doubled over together, hands on knees and I watched Harold pant, saw the sweat drip and blood drying in tiny bubbles on his hands. He looked at me and he was still smiling.

We walked the roads back toward Harold's and neither of us spoke. The sun was low and it was a chore just to keep my legs moving as we passed through patches of sunlight and shadow. Harold seemed unaffected and I struggled to stay with him. I slapped at mosquitoes absently, scratched their bites until I bled. All I could think about was that mutilated hand, Bryan's face as he screamed out. Harold looked wood carved, sweaty and stoic. I was scared. I'd be implicated in this, just because I was there. I thought about my dad, he wouldn't leave me blameless. I thought about Harold's dad. The salamanders would be nothing compared to what we'd done. I tried to say that we should run away, that I needed to and that I needed Harold with me to do it. The words wouldn't come and I just followed my friend, used his momentum to catch whatever was coming.

The police were already in Harold's driveway as we approached the big house, the dream house. I felt like running again when I saw the police cruiser, but I was tethered to Harold, bound by the act we'd committed, a pair of criminals already in cuffs. Harold didn't slow his pace at the sight of the car and I wondered how long we'd be in juvie, if I'd have to see Dad before then.

As we hit the edge of the yard, Harold's mom hit the front door, crossed the yard and ran down the drive to meet us, crying for Harold. Her car remained where it had been and I knew she should have been at work. The distance between Harold's mom and me seemed to be unbridgeable, like some timeless, spaceless void where beings saw each other, moved toward one another, but were never quite able to reach. It was a hell and I saw the hand again, the last finger falling away and I knew it was what I deserved. As she took Harold into her arms I saw the ambulance, partially hidden by the curve in the blacktop and the purple dogwood that had just begun dropping its leaves. Did they bring Bryan here? Evidence of what we'd done in case we tried to deny it? I watched Harold's mom hold him, as if answering a prayer, she pulled him in and clutched him so tight it was as if she was trying to squeeze all the pain and fear and guilt out of him. I stood so close I smelled the mixture of the potato soup and vomit on her. She cried and her breath was sour and I did not want to move away. I wanted her to pull me into her. Harold and I looked at each other, his ear to a breast, mine to the wind, ringing. She held him close, kept him womb warm, her heart beating out the remembered rhythms of black sleep. And just for a moment I saw us burying the frogs properly.

Human Zoo

I asked Jane how she felt about the human zoo.

"It's a travesty. It's a cultural abortion. It's disgusting."

It was all those things. "You want to go?"

"Yeah," she said. "I could use some disgusting."

Dad loaned me the car when I told him I was taking Jane. He put the keys in my palm. He put a handful of change in my other hand.

"To feed the animals," he said.

Jane smoked cigarettes all the way to the zoo. She cracked the window barely and flicked ash into the wind. She burned the roof of the wagon in at least seven different places. "Sorry," she said each time, but she didn't use any more caution than she had before. It was rainy and the Grand River was flooded almost twenty feet onto the shore. Trees rose from the water like they were meant for life in the swamp. The waste that flowed through the river was creeping up toward the highway and the smell mixed with the cigarette smoke. I breathed in deep to get a trace of Jane. The stink never stuck to her. She didn't even smell of grease, though she worked just as many hours in the kitchen as I did. I was now a reeking mess of lard fumes and cigarette smoke and river stench. Jane flicked a butt out the window. Of course it hit the door frame before exiting, raining a shower of tiny orange cherry specks and leaving black pinhole burns on the seat. I watched in the rearview for a methane explosion. Something violent that would ignite the whole river, adding the smell of burning rubber as the old fishermen in their waders burned away to nothing. It didn't happen and I looked over at her. She felt my eyes and met them.

"What?"

"Nothing." And I wondered how she pulled thoughts out of me by the handful and threw them against some giant white canvas, exposing the ridiculous in me in vivid detail.

"Want one?" she said holding out the pack, showing me the cancer-ridden pancreas on the front.

"Sure." Maybe I'd have better luck setting the fire.

We entered the zoo. The place was gray and dead. The cold wind met us head on through every twist and turn of the concrete path. Family units found us with their gaze, a polite smile creeping up on defeated lips.

At the fowl pond the convicts sat in the cooling water naked, their necks collared in leather and chained to the rock façade behind them. They were mostly foreigners, not the hostiles, but those who had tried to stay after the big border wall closed for good. They'd been warned. It was almost ten years now, but the ads had been everywhere: The Man himself on the tube and telling them, "go home. We don't want you here anymore. Go back to where you came from." I guessed the fowl pond was full of these hangers-on because they just wouldn't leave, and now they were chained up in the water and their fingers were cut off, a symbolic wing clipping that prevented them from leaving if they wanted to. Jane and I watched them. They looked pathetic sitting in their own filth, waiting to catch some water-borne illness and die, flat fingerless hands stroking the water for comfort.

I used the change Dad had given me and I bought a dollar's worth of feed from the coin-op machine, twisting the handle and getting a handful for fifty cents. I gave some to Jane and we tossed it into the dirty water, watched the captives climb all over each other for the scraps of waterlogged bran or whatever meal it was. They tried to gouge out each other's eyes with phantom fingers. They cried out in squawks as we walked away. Even with tongues cut out and vocal cords scraped raw and scarred, they still tried to speak.

It was the same type of scene throughout. On monkey island the naked residents shivered, their hands cut off and sewn on their ankles. The reptile house with snake people stripped of their limbs. All the habitats that once housed a big cat or wolf or wolverine, they were filled with chained people who were hostile in some way or another. The aquarium was packed full of men and women and kids, underwater, just enough air above the surface to poke up a nostril or lips and take a breath before being yanked down by the next beast struggling for breath and trying to keep the dead at bay lest they float up and squat below the most valuable real estate.

Jane and I rested on a glossy, plastic bench fashioned to look like a log. Across from us was the tiger habitat. The man inside paced behind the glass, back and forth, licking his chops, growling. The info plaque stated he was a rebel, a dissident responsible for the deaths of over fifty wall-builders. His fate was the smashing of his pelvis and femurs, never puzzled back together, giving him no choice but to move like the stalking big cat he'd resembled in life. Two young zookeepers walked by on patrol, hands on their assault rifles. They paid us little mind. Jane watched them walk by.

"I wanted to get assigned here," she said.

"I thought you said it was 'disgusting.'"

"I know. Maybe that's why. Because they wouldn't have me. I came here a lot when I was a kid. Lots of people on our side of the glass. Now this. It doesn't feel right, does it?"

"I wouldn't want to be here," I said. "But they have to go somewhere. We let them walk the street and it's chaos."

She laughed.

"You know what I mean." I said. "More chaos. These people did something to get here."

"Maybe. But what if they had succeeded? It might be us. They're victims of their politics."

"We all are, I think."

She thought about that. "Maybe. But to live this life? What warrants that?"

I read the large plaque hung above. "Treason. Murder." I pointed to the pacing animal. "In his case."

Jane nodded. She stood and moved to the enclosure, climbed over the metal rail and put her cheek to the glass. The man stopped pacing, rested in front of her. Jane stroked the length of his body, again and again, hand squeaking on the glass. And I envied the tiger man. If given the order I'd break him all over again.

"Let's go," I said. Something in my tone pulled her away, anger that maybe she mistook for confidence, safe and separate from my rival by four inches of reinforced glass. Jane smiled, still stroking the broken cat, that man, but looking at me. I again wondered how she had the ability to expose me to myself. I didn't know what she wanted from me: a companion, a partner in commiseration, honesty with someone other than the mirror. How could I have known anything else? She was Jane and she was beautiful and she moved me in a way that made me think the end of the world was my idea. That's a gift. To let a man think his destruction is his own doing. But that was her gift. She was my Jane.

No, just Jane.

The Yard Sale

The young girl, his choice, sat bored and hot on the front porch as he melted in the desert sun. Laid out before him on the borrowed card tables was an amalgam of domestic goods, female things, baby toys. He made change, hot quarter dollars burning his fingertips, stealing their sensitivity, toughening them. He wondered why he had sold the patio umbrella.

"How much for the high chair?"

"20 dollars."

"Take 5?"

"Okay." He was defeated, tired of haggling with strangers who couldn't take history into account when assessing value. It was robbery, but then, he just wanted the stuff gone.

He looked back at the young girl. She looked innocent and sexy as she shook her water glass, entertaining herself with clinking ice cubes. He watched a messy child rifle through the box of small plush animals, making them sticky. The child's mother said nothing and they bought nothing. His phone rang from the porch.

"It's yours," the young girl said to him.

"Will you get it?"

The girl looked at the display. "It's your wife."

"Answer it." He left the tables and walked up to the porch. Cars continued to park, blocking the driveway, the road. Horns and voices went off behind him. He took the phone from the beautiful girl.

"Hi," he said into the phone.

"Is that her?" His wife asked.

"Yes," he said. The guilt returned, but then he remembered to be angry. "Are you with him?"

"Yes." She said. Her anger became guilt. "How's the sale?"

"It's hot out here."

"I'm sure. Sorry I bailed on you."

"It's okay."

"No it's not. It isn't fair."

"Don't worry about it. No reason we both should suffer."

"I guess not."

He stood silent, looked at the fat man holding the folded playpen. The man was waving for his attention. He nodded to the man.

"I should go," he said into the phone.

"Call me if there's anything left. I'll put it on our sale next weekend."

"Okay, you'll come by?"

"Yes."

"Okay. I'll call if there's anything left and you can come by."

"Yes." The dead air was heavy and familiar; it stole his mind from the heat. He looked down at the girl who looked up at him with unspoiled brown eyes, curious eyes with no frame of reference. She'd been spared the hardships and tragedies that befall married couples, parents, thus far anyway. But she was playing the game. Her turn would come.

"Talk to you then. Bye." He set the phone on the small patio table and the girl took his hand.

"You need a shower," she said. "Now." Her grin and eyes were as irresistible as they had been the first time he saw her. He stroked her black hair and looked over his shoulder. The activity of the yard sale had lulled to a quiet nothing. The man with the playpen had gone away empty-handed, protesting the quality of the customer service.

Under the cool beading streams of water, she washed him and then he washed her. On his knees he ran the cloth up and down one soft leg, then the other. He lathered the stems with shaving cream from a pink can and then gently ran the razor up and down their length. He wiped away the excess cream and continued to stroke the slick silk, massaged the firm calf. She coaxed him to her with a small hand holding his chin. They kissed under the piped-in rain. He pulled her to him, into him, and she pulled in return, him into her. They moved together. Her head fell back and he held the small of her arched back, he kissed her neck. His own body shook as the girl moaned and purred. When it was done, they held each other and he nibbled her earlobe.

They dried one another and moved to the bedroom, damp and naked. He would collect the remains from the yard and call his wife in the morning and she would come to get those remains. She'd collect the baby's things. He thought about throwing them away, lying, telling her they'd sold for a fair price.

Maybe they would talk. Maybe they would forget about everything and fall back into their old habits.

He put on the same pair of ripped jeans over fresh underwear. He watched the young girl dress and could not help being excited by her body as she put on her own underclothes, exotic and still unfamiliar, silky as her skin. She lay on the bed and flipped through a celebrity magazine. He knew the young girl was more than a habit, but not yet an addiction. She could become one. Part of him wanted that.

He stepped out into the sun and didn't notice anything was amiss until he was halfway down the driveway. His eyes adjusted to the sun and he saw it was gone, everything except the empty folding tables, which looked back at him with callousness, wearing a thin layer of desert dust. He cursed his inattentiveness. He cursed the thieves and then he cursed his wife. He may not have been there, but neither was she. Her reason for coming back to the house was stolen, loaded into some deadbeat's pick-up truck with the rest of the sale. He left the tables where they sat and let them bake in the heat, let the dust layer thicken. He wanted the girl to still be on the bed when he went back inside.

Tu's Chicken

I used to kill small animals with my dad and an old .22 when I was a kid. They were rodents, mostly muskrats, but occasionally I'd put a new hole in a bird or a feral cat. Dad would lead me out of town on the west bound train route and smoke giant cigars while he talked about god's plans, plans that included reducing the number of muskrats living along the tracks.

"Vermin," he'd say as I picked one off. "They'd shoot you if they had a trigger finger." We never went on an actual hunting trip because Dad was away too much. He drove a truck full of office furniture back and forth between Ashville and Omaha. Our big game was the muskrats.

Dad had killed four people in his life. The first ones I learned about were some kids in a VW bus in Iowa. Dad was getting back on the highway after stopping at a Flying J's for dinner. The kids ran the signal at the onramp and he clipped their rear bumper when they cut him off. The bus rolled down the slope from the onramp to the highway below. I don't know if the fall killed them, but another rig demolished the van at 70 miles per hour. The kids' families sued the company Dad drove for and lost. They had to pay the company's legal expenses after another civil trial. Dad testified to the circumstances for the second time while the parents cried and wished they'd left well enough alone, if you can consider having dead kids "well enough." That was two of the four people dad killed.

Dad said one person had it coming. The truck was his weapon of non-choice once again. He had parked his rig in the lot of a closed Wal-Mart in southern Illinois to get some sleep. He told me he was dreaming about hammering railroad ties into place with giant spikes and a sledge. He said I was in the dream. Dad hammered the ties while I followed and shot muskrats. He said I kept asking why their families didn't cry. He told me to "just shoot." He woke up and the shots stopped, but the hammering continued. He said the sound scared him so bad he couldn't move. I never knew my dad to be scared of anything and the comment filled my belly with his fear. Dad peaked out of the sleeper and saw a figure through the driver's side glass. It was holding a *Rambo*-style survival knife and hitting the window with the compass end. Dad hopped into the seat wearing only his forty-inch-waist white Hanes and fumbled with the keys in the dark. The figure said something Dad couldn't understand and the tapping outside became a frenzied staccato. Dad found the ignition and the rig shook. It snorted and bucked the figure off. Dad said the thump you'd expect when you ran over someone was more of a wet squish. The figure screamed until the 3rd or 4th set of set of tires. No one sued that time.

Dad liked to tell me about life during our murderous jaunts down the tracks.

"Don't marry a Catholic."

"Why not?"

"You like meat on Fridays?"

"Yeah."

"Don't marry a Catholic."

My mom was a Catholic. We ate fish on Fridays. I figured Mom just liked cooking fish or she did it because Dad was overweight and one lean meal a week was better than nothing. I didn't see how fish wasn't meat.

"Don't trust the police."

"Why not?"

"'Cause they're assholes."

Dad was a cop before he drove truck. When I was about 6 years old, I'd get up real early and wait for his cruiser to pull up the driveway. It was always dark when I went out to meet him. He'd pick me up and his gun would grind into my hip. He'd tell me about all the bad guys he caught while he tucked me back into bed. I had a lot of nightmare about criminals, but they always ended happily because my dad would shoot them. I found out later that Dad was let go because he was caught drunk driving. He became belligerent with the cop who stopped him and tried to take the officer's sidearm. He was allowed to plead down to disorderly conduct if he'd resign. He said people don't look out for each other like they should.

The last person I learned he killed was in Vietnam. He didn't talk about being there very often so when he did I listened. He said he probably got a lot of them, but it was always under chaotic circumstances so you never really knew. You just shot.

"His name was Tu, but we called him Bruce Lee because he knew kung fu. He wasn't a VC."

"What's a VC?"

"A bad guy in Vietnam. Tu was a little shit, but I watched him fight some kids and he held his own real good. Five boys bigger than him and he took them all on. He was quick. He'd step it back when it got too hairy and then tagged anyone fool enough to get close. He could spin and throw his leg high enough to kick any of them taller boys in the mouth. The guys and me just stood back 'til he started taking the worst of it. Like I said, it was five on one."

"He couldn't win?"

"He did win."

"But you helped him."

"Yeah, but he fought and kept his chicken. He could have gave it up without a fight. Wasn't his fault we chased them other kids off. It was his circumstances."

"Was it his pet chicken?"

"His family had a farm. It was probably for eggs."

"I don't like eggs. I'd eat the chicken."

"I know you would. We saw Tu back to his house in case them kids came back and there were some VCs there."

"The bad guys."

"Right, they were always interrogating, looking for spies. We come out of the bush into the small farm clearing and there's 3 of them slapping Tu's daddy. Tu screamed and ran to him, dropped the chicken. The VCs turned and shot him like nothing and then bayoneted his belly. We fired and they fired and in the end they all went down. No way to know whose bullet made what hole. Tu was on the ground just howlin'. They stirred his pot pretty good with the bayonet and his insides were a mess. Our medic was already dead a few days and we didn't know how to fix Tu, if he could be fixed. He just kept screaming and bleeding. The chicken was running in circles round the yard, eating bugs and pecking at the bodies. Tu's daddy picked himself up and came running and yelled something and a lady come out of the thatch shack, Tu's mom I suspect. They sat by him and were praying I guess, chanting some nonsense, and they kept saying something to us. We figured they wanted help, but there was nothing we could do. Tu is still screaming his head off. Finally his daddy gets up and walks right up to me. He points to the barrel of my gun and then runs back to Tu and starts tapping on the boy's forehead. He points to me and then taps on Tu's forehead again."

"He wanted you to shoot him."

"I know."

"Did you?"

"Yes."

The Tree House

Though all four of the young men had a hand in building the tree house, it looked very alien to the three standing on the ground. And he, their confused friend thirty feet above, looked equally alien, staring down with humoring eyes, as if he were seeing them for what they truly were. They were his friends, but in their heart they felt betrayed, felt that he was belittling each of them by living this fantasy with the same conviction one gives a desperate truth.

The three on the ground had names: there was Marcus, the future veterinarian; Abe, the future MBA; and Scott, the future lawyer. Each of them stared up, up, up through the sycamores, squinting in the bright sunshine that backlit the tree house. They had come to retrieve Ernie.

He'd climbed up there the night of their high school graduation, eschewing the parties in preference of a new solitude. He had remained there for over three months and as far as anyone knew he had not come down, not once. He stayed all hours in the branches reading books, watching network television on a small black-and-white set, hunting squirrels, masturbating, and when an idea would come, writing. Ernie self-published his stories or poems in the form of a wadded paper ball or a folded airplane. To those around him – his mother, his father, the ineffectual police and fire departments, and now his three childhood friends come to rescue him from himself - the scribblings were the work of either a madman or an obstinate child.

Ernie, stood out on the front porch of the tree house, conversing in shouts and amplified gestures.

"Come down, Ernie." Marcus said. "This isn't healthy."

"What's not healthy?"

"This, what you're doing. What have you been eating?"

"Squirrels mostly. I have some tomatoes and peppers growing in pots on the roof."

"Water?"

"I filter the rain, but I have the garden hose up here as a back up."

It was as if he spoke it into existence at that moment, the three on the ground pulled the snaking green hose out of the background with their eyes, following it first from the base of the tree and up to the tree house and then back down again and out of the clearing, back to the house of his parents, a structure invisible save for the breeze that occasionally raised the veil of the minty willows that surrounded them.

"C'mon, Ernie, still." Marcus said. "You got something wrong with your head? You depressed?"

"No, maybe just-" he searched his personal lexicon for the proper term; he believed the word found in the thesaurus was never correct, "just dissatisfied, disillusioned, apathetic. I don't know, but that's got nothing to do with my being up here. I want to be up here. I just want to live in the tree house."

"You can't," Scott said. "Your folks want you to come down. It's their house. You should listen to them."

"Why?"

"Because it's their property for one. You can't just squat here your whole life. And if that doesn't stir you, maybe an appeal to your emotions will: they're worried about you. We all are."

"There's nothing to worry about," Ernie said. "Everybody just needs to let it go. I know what I'm doing. I've been up here for three months. I'm fine. Never better!"

Abe retrieved and unfurled a wad of paper. He read out loud:

"...and he stood up and stabbed his mother in the face with her crochet needle, the unfinished winter scarf still attached and trailing out of the room after her like a gymnast's ribbon, a visual manifestation of her screams."

"It's a story. Like it?"

"Your mom crochets," Scott said.

"A lot of moms crochet," Ernie said. "Some dads too. Some people who never had any kids. It's a story!"

Abe crumpled the paper and let it fall back to the ground. "Look man, college? Don't you remember all the plans we made for college? We were all going to rush the same frats, room together all four years, get laid? How you going to get laid up there?"

"Any girl worth screwing will find her way up here."

"That's nuts," Abe said. "And what about money? Don't you want to join the real world and make some money?"

"I don't need money." Ernie climbed atop the railing and the three on the ground had the same thoughts: first that he was coming down, then that maybe he was going to jump, commit suicide or at least cripple himself. They saw the pellet gun slung over his shoulder as he walked the salvaged, scrap-pile two-by-four with dirty bare feet and hoisted himself up into the branches of the tall sycamore. He moved smoothly, like a monkey on the swaying, creaking branches, moving comfortably, smoothly, nearly gliding on dexterous feet. He climbed higher and roosted in the crotch of a large limb. He took aim and fired the rifle. Poot.

"Ha!" Ernie said. "Got him." Ernie climbed even higher and reached into a net of woven bark strips just below the empty space he'd sighted with the gun. He retrieved the twitching, injured squirrel from the net and broke its neck with a quick twist of his hands.

"I bait them with acorns," Ernie said. "I'm completely self-sufficient. Nearly." He lowered himself back to the porch of the tree house and tossed the squirrel through the open door. Again, reality was carved from a raw slab and the three young men saw the ground was littered with squirrel remains, skin and fur and bones in varying degrees of decay.

"Ernie," Marcus said, "you're sick! Really man! Sick!" Scott touched him on the shoulder to both comfort and quiet him, for Ernie's sake.

"You're not sick, Ernie." Scott said. "We just want you to come down and live life with us. Like it's supposed to be lived."

Ernie laughed. The sound was not the boy they'd grown up with, but the cackling chortle of an old man. "Why can't you just let me be? I don't come around and try to get you guys to do anything. Go to school, join the frat! Get laid and paid! I wish you the best! Just let me be!"

"But this isn't living!" Marcus said.

"Then I must be dead," Ernie said. He laughed again and went inside the tree house. The three listened as he banged around inside the retreat, still laughing. They looked to each other and were certain that their young friend had truly lost it. Ernie came back scribbling on a sheet of paper. He smiled on the words as a father does a child, a man soaked in the pride of creation. He folded the paper into a plane and released it into the world. The plane glided and circled, spiraling in the sunlight before nose-diving and landing at the feet of the three.

"Read it." Ernie said.

Scott picked up the plane, made it paper again and read:

"They come to right me. To live is to come down, down. Then I must be dead." He let the paper fall. "A poem?"

"A haiku. What do you think?"

"I think it's shit." Marcus said. Scott punched his shoulder hard.

"It's great, Ernie." Scott said. "Best I've ever read." He looked at Abe.

"Yeah," Abe said, "Yeah, it's, real deep, Ernie. You just came up with that right now?"

"Yeah." Ernie's face had fallen so low they could nearly touch it. "Marcus said it was shit though."

Scott and Abe looked at Marcus, waiting on him to retract his review.

Marcus didn't look at them. He stared at Ernie. "I did say that. Because it *is* shit." Scott and Abe tried to hush him, but he stepped closer to the tree, facing Ernie alone. "Let this crazy bastard live up in the trees if he wants to. What do we care?"

"C'mon," Abe said. "He's a friend."

"Ooh, high school friends. Big deal. Like any of us are going to be friends in four years anyway. If we are, I'll fucking shoot myself!"

"Marcus," Scott said, "what the hell's the matter with you?"

"Screw you, man. I want to grow. I want to leave all of this in the past. This whole town. I don't want to think about it ever again. Rearview mirror, man." His hard eyes shifted between the two on the ground, stabbed Ernie in the tree. "Why won't you just come out of the tree you crazy bastard?"

"Why do you need me to so bad?" Ernie asked, chewing on some sundried squirrel jerky.

"Because that's what grown-ups do! You need all this attention! Like you're so special. 'Look at me! Look at me!' The world is the way it is, and it isn't about living in a goddamn tree for your whole life killing squirrels! Deal with it!"

"I never asked you to come here! You showed up on your own. All of you!"

"So write a story about it asshole!" Marcus looked to Scott and Abe for approval. Neither spoke and then it suddenly began raining on Marcus alone.

"Sorry," Ernie said, "latrine's full." A soft piece of stool landed on Marcus' piss-drenched head. The soggy feces formed to his dome like a little hat.

Marcus tried to speak, but his rage reduced him to only piss spittle and tears. He ran from the clearing, away from the tree house and his friends.

Ernie and the two on the ground looked at one another. No one knew quite how to continue. And then Abe began to giggle.

"Did you see that shit? It stuck to his head!" Abe couldn't continue. The laughter grew until it had him fully. "Ernie," He choked, "you are nasty, man!"

"Ernie, you are one sick fool!" Scott said, trying to scold, but the laughter got him too. It was just like when they were twelve years old and Marcus, the go to butt of the joke, was sent home crying once again.

"That Marcus," Abe could barely speak, "he's su-, su- he's such shit head!" And the three friends laughed until they were crying.

"Oh, hilarious," Marcus said as he crashed back into the clearing. "A goddamn riot! I'll get that dumb bastard down." He was holding an ax. Ernie leaned over the railing.

"Don't you do it! Don't you do it! I'll kill you!"

"Come down and stop me!" Marcus said. He swung the ax, splintering wood flying about his madman grin, dirt and bark sticking in his teeth. He swung the tool again and again.

Scott touched his shoulder for a third time. "Easy man, c'mon!" Marcus turned and swung the ax hard, splitting Scott's face like a log. Scott fell and the ax came free from his face with the sound of a wet kiss. Marcus looked at Abe who was already making a run for it and then Marcus was after him, their feet crunching in the brush and debris. For a moment it was quiet. Ernie stared at the ground, listening to the wind, seeing nothing but Scott's corpse bleeding on top of all the paper and squirrel remains and latrine waste. Abe's screams broke the silence and then just as quickly, the quiet returned. Marcus appeared in the clearing, blood spattered and panting, looking demon strong with the ax in his hands, like that paper towel lumber jack in his blood beard and wet, red shirt. He began chopping at the tree again, painting the pulpy gash with blood from the ax blade.

"Marcus!" Ernie screamed down at him. "Marcus! Marcus! Don't you do it, Marcus! Don't you do it!" Marcus gave no indication of hearing the plea. He chopped. Ernie grabbed his paper and a pencil. He scribbled out a story in what little time he might have left. It was pretty good too.

Dig It?

I asked her to stay and she said, "Can't, daddy."

I asked her why not and she said, "Can't. Daddy." But before she hit the bricks she leaned and arched her back over the e-brake. Her feet hit the concrete as her kitty cat tongue scratched my cheek.

"Don't wreck," she said.

"Baby, this fool done already crashed."

Dogs Don't Know No Jesus

He woke up when he heard the howling, but by the time he made it into the backyard the wounded coyote was jumping over the fence and Ben was nearly dead. The dog laid panting, his neck fur red and wet. Ben was big and strong, and though there was a time when he would have whipped three coyotes, this wasn't it. The severed ear in his mouth was only a testament to his past.

When Mom woke, they buried Ben together. The ground was rocky and it took most of morning, both of them stabbing, to complete the hole. It was a good hole, deep and wide and layered with mini strata of lesser time. The boy rolled Ben with his foot and the dog landed with a hollow thud. As they shoveled dirt back into the hole he said to Mom, "Careful of his eyes."

After lunch time, Mom went to work. She left him on the couch watching his cartoons, but as soon as she was out the door he went to her room. He pulled open her top drawer and sifted through various pieces of lingerie until he found the military-issue nine millimeter Daddy had left him. The gun wasn't his yet, not until he was grown, but he liked to take it out when Mom was gone and point it at himself in the mirror. He played both victim and criminal at once, feeling power and fear. Sometimes he loaded the gun, and one time he discharged it accidently, put a hole in the bedroom wall next to the family portrait. His Daddy was dressed in his Blues in the picture and Mom's hair was longer and he himself was barely more than a baby. The boy moved the old picture over a few inches and Mom never noticed.

The gun discharged on Daddy once too, when he was cleaning it. The boy came home from school and found Daddy in the bedroom, bled out and dead, the oil and rag next to him. The boy watched TV until Mom returned from work that night. He didn't know what else to do.

He took the gun from Mom's room and put it into his canvas backpack. He made three ham sandwiches, drained the remains from a gallon of milk and rinsed the container, refilled it with water from the leaky kitchen tap. The boy took the pack and went into the backyard, toward the fence, careful to avoid the new grave. He hopped the fence same as the coyote and turned to the right, down the dirt alley where he picked up the dry wash that lead into the desert.

He walked for the remainder of the day and as the air chilled he spotted the fire, never feeling the cold. It was a man, somewhere between twenty and forty years in the boy's eyes. The man gave a start when he saw him approach, cursed him, but then asked the boy to sit. The man shared a can of beans and the boy shared a sandwich. The man drank milky agave alcohol from a jar and offered some to the boy, but he declined. The boy sat silent as the man rocked back and forth, drinking and occasionally laughing at the fire, showing his mouthful of broken teeth.

"What else you got in the pack?" he asked later.

"My gun," the boy said.

"Can I see it?" the man said. The boy pulled out the piece, held it up. It shone silver in the moonlight. "Can I hold it?"

"No. You can't." The boy thanked the man for the trade and walked further down the wash. It was dark but for the moon and he could hear the man laughing for a long time. When the laughter ceased, he tucked himself away in a dense patch of thorny mesquite scrub, and then he felt the cold. Coyotes howled over a kill and the boy knew he was going in the right direction.

The boy woke shivering in the sun and walked to warm himself. He allowed himself a sip of water and half of a sandwich. He hoped to find the coyote that day, but if wishes had value his Daddy would not have shot himself in the head and Ben would be alive. He left the wash and went in the direction of the howling. He walked until there was no sign of where he'd been, only raw desert in every direction, framed on the compass points by the ranges that surrounded the valley. The boy looked behind himself and identified the peak by which he'd find his way home. He pressed on and as cold as he'd been in the night was as hot as he was by midday. He removed his shirt and fashioned a sloppy turban. Hours later his torso was red and stinging hot. He put the shirt back on and left his face to burn.

He finished the water well before sunset, thought briefly of returning home, but he stumbled on, hearing coyotes ahead of him, coaxing him forward, and then hearing the dogs in every direction, and seeing strange men with fiery teeth, broken and spilling laughter into the dust. Ben trotted at his side, neck open and pulsing blood, the coyote's ear between his teeth. The boy fell, tried to collect enough saliva to convince his dry mouth it didn't ache for water. He tasted dirt and saw the moon rising. The coyotes howled and he knew they were coming for him. He found the gun in his pack and held the cool steel to his face. He searched the darkness for movement. He smelled for the blood of his coyote.

Shaved

I met a girl on Drummond Island who had an old broken down school bus in her yard. She said there was a kid's head in it. She wouldn't let me see it because her daddy didn't want anyone in there. She told me she lived on the island year round and didn't ever wear underwear.

The clapboard house she lived in with Daddy lost the fight with time; white paint peeled and gave way to green, molded lumber. It looked malnourished, lonely in the middle of the big yard.

She took me to the garbage dump one night while the rest of my family roasted hotdogs and her Daddy was at the only tavern on the island. We stopped in on him and he gave a fiver and seven cigarettes and a smack on the ass. We stopped at the general store for hotdogs of our own, four packages. I chipped in a buck.

We fed two black bears at the dump, lured them in with the hotdogs. When we ran out, the bears came closer and we scrambled up the side of the dump and the bears went back to rooting through the trash. We sat up atop the pit and I fingered her, the first girl I ever did it to. I asked her why she had no pubes and she laughed at me and called me a dummy. She told me to rub her clit, not just jam my fingers up there. She helped me find it and then she gave me my first girl hand job and it was the most glorious experience of my life. I got hard for months whenever I thought about it.

I missed her for a long time, but when I didn't anymore I started to wonder how many other boys she'd been with and if they were as stupid as me to believe her about the head in the bus and if they thought of her whenever they shaved.

Presents in Lieu of Child Support

My little brother was born on X-mas. Dad said he must have been Santa's baby because the kid sure as hell wasn't his. Then Dad left. I remember being so mad at Santa for screwing up my family that I took all the presents labeled with my name and burned them out in the back yard. To this day I associate the smell of lighter fluid and melting plastic with snow and X-mas.

By the next holiday season, my little brother was one and Mom was dating a man who looked nothing like Santa. His name was Warren, and he regarded me with enthusiasm in front of my mother, but when we were left alone the conversation stopped. Even at six, I felt the awkwardness of the silence and took it upon myself to force conversation. I first felt that way with Dad when I was old enough to remember getting smacked. I didn't fear Warren the same way, but masculine silence was still a hole I felt something wicked might usurp if I didn't speak.

"Want to see my cars?" I said.

He said no and that was just fine because six months earlier, the last time I talked to my father on the telephone I burned them up because they too were from Santa.

"Want to play Mousetrap?"

"No kid. I want to watch the game."

It was an old game on cable. It was U of M versus Ohio State University. Or as he called it, *The* Ohio State University

"C'mon, Bucks!" Warren said. Ours was a Michigan house when Dad was here. Later when Mom asked me how I liked Warren I told her I didn't.

"Why not?" she said. Toby was at her breast, sucking away like an illegitimate piglet.

"Cause he likes the Fuckeyes," I said. And then I waited to get smacked because I knew "fuck" was one of the worst words you could say. But she didn't hit me. She got glassy-eyed and smiled. She looked down at my little brother on her tit and then back at me.

"You sound just like him," she said and switched Toby to the other side. The indignant wail gave way to the sucking and slurping.

Did I make that much noise back then? I imagined myself on mother's tit, drinking quietly.

* * *

It was right before X-mas break. Somebody out on the playground said Santa wasn't real and these other kids were saying he was, and pretty soon it was two camps screaming back and forth. I came along and Trevor Fries asks me where I stood and I said, "stand on what?"

And he said, "You believe in Santa Claus, don't you?"

The question was absurd to me. My little brother existed because Santa existed. My dad left because Santa existed.

"Yeah," I said. "That asshole is real. And I'm going to kill him this year."

"Why you wanna kill Santa for?" Little Fisher asked. He was Little Fisher because his older brother was held back a year and was in the same class and he was Big Fisher.

"I got my reasons," I said. I had heard that simple rationale in a movie once and I liked the way it sounded coming out of my mouth.

Even a Face Can Be a Canvas

I ask people: what did they call a mountain before people came along and gave them a name? I'm not talking the Rockies or Smokeys or Andes or Himalayas, but those handles just further illustrate what I'm getting at. My point is that once upon a time, before we told these stories, everything just ran into everything else; tree and ground were the same thing, same with mountains and valleys, earth and sky were one thing. I see the little animals running around before we called them mammals or birds or frogs or whatever, it was truth. And that's what I'm telling her when this guy starts shooting off his mouth.

"Sounds like a bunch of shit. What you drinkin', darlin'?" I look at him but he only looks at her, and she has this kind of rescued look on her face. Usually I'd be embarrassed, but the alcohol is working and it just makes me madder than hell.

"She's drinkin' the beer I just bought her."

"Oh, my mistake," he says. He pulls out a wad of bills and lays down a twenty next to the dollar I was saving for the tip jar. "How about I buy your round here and you go take a walk, In the mountains, maybe?" He laughs and she smiles and his buddies move in, smelling like a busted bottle of cologne.

"No thanks." I say. I turn to her and I think she is pleasantly surprised I didn't take the walk, or that she just likes the drama, and in the back of my mind I watch the drunk part of me from a corner and I go on.

"So back to the point: we're all artists. To be human is to be an artist. The complex web of meaning and symbols we manage to weave every second of every day."

"What the fuck are you talking about?" one of the hyenas says. I don't acknowledge him, but I elaborate.

"Without language, the world is nothing but a formless, shapeless blob. We carve out meaning with our words. We create our worlds!" I down the last of my beer and slam my mug on the bar for emphasis. The tender gives me a look like he would crack my head open if it were that kind of place and I put up a finger for one more. "You want another?" I ask the girl, but she's slid off the stool and she's leaving with the other guy, and his friends are looking over their shoulders, laughing at me. The bartender comes over and puts down the beer. "Last one. Then beat it, huh?" I feel indignant, but I concede with a nod and I turn my attentions to the drink. I try not to hear the guy mocking me from the large corner booth. I look at the twenty and wave the bartender back. I slide the bill forward and thumb back to my new friends. "Set them up with one on me."

I don't make it ten feet out of the place and I'm puking my guts out in the parking lot. It seems like I'm there forever when I hear footsteps.

"Hey! The artist! That's quite a masterpiece you're working on." He got the girl and he still isn't satisfied.

I look up from my retch and see him and her and them, all smiles.

"Laugh and mock, but I speak the truth."

"You speak shit."

"Ever heard of Sartre?" I ask wiping my mouth with my sleeve.

"Ever heard of fucking off?"

They all laugh again and I stand straight and stumble forward, put a hand on his shoulder. He shakes me off and gives me a good push that sends me ass first into my own wet filth. I don't move until I see him taking his jacket off and handing it to one of the group. I try to scramble up and he slugs me hard in the gut and I dry heave. He swings again and catches me in the jaw.

"C'mon. Throw a punch," he says. I swing wild, lunging and I miss. He hits me in the nose and breaks it. It doesn't hurt but I know it's crushed, because I heard it and I can't see for the tears and I taste blood. I feel an arm drape around my neck and it starts to squeeze. I slap at the limb, try to pry it off but it doesn't move. I hear warped laughter as I drop to my knees. Everything is black, foreground and background merging, no division. My hand slaps the pavement, finds something hard, something loose. I create it out of nothing. I give it a name and then they believe.

In Love like a Parvo Puppy

Death is a selfish act and that's why everyone does it. You will have no excuse when you don't. And you'll think about this fact every time you're finger fucked, with every grimy digit tunneling into your special wet. And you'll think it's pleasant, like a bleeding relief worth a few hundred dollars. And still raw from his touch, you'll get home push that button again and again, while his friends sniff his fist and he thinks about nothing. If you light yourself on fire your mother will join a TV panel discussion. Her hair and make-up will be perfect. And the episode will win an Emmy, but you'll still be the girl of his jack off nightmares. And forever you're going to be special, so tangy, so green. Remember, you only get one first time. So try everything once, twice if we're talking acid. And just like that song about how many times you were a lady, a bowling ball has the same number of fuckable holes.

Pulp

She sits and rips skin from bone, fleshy truth. She devours the orange, laughs, flips her hair. Does she know she is my daymare?

I watch her. I finger the lunch table's scars: "mike is a faget", "alicia luvs chris." Her eyes flicker like a simile that's like, I don't know, something else?

We rise upon orders from the bell. Old habits are unmurderable. I watch with dry orbs that linger only long enough to make me sweat, scanning to assure I'm not unwrapped by another. Her sunshine mingles among clouded peers. She hides from eyes that would stare until blindness.

I write sad poems in my room, bold-font verses that die with a keystroke whenever someone appears.

"Can I get some help? I don't get it. How do I balance this?" We ask the same questions.

The answer is easy.

"Put a 'two' in front of that oxygen. There you go."

She smiles and I want to tell her that she has flesh stuck in her teeth. But to tell her is to free that bit of pulp, a tawdry liberation by her purple, tooth-ravaged nails, and then to see it dropped to the floor, or at best, swallowed. My secret no longer. A non-thing. Indigestible roughage. It's a pathetic parallel. It's forced poetry.

I read books that put it eloquently. Books with titles you could never have thought of yourself. My book is called Letch. Letch me teach you something about red ink: it's my seed.

Easy

I stand outside of bars and wait for fights that don't happen. But if they did. Oh boy if they did, sir, let me tell you. I'd take that Jake character, the one with the leather and motorcycle. I'd take that Jake character and boy would I whoop him good. I'd find a chain in the alley - no, I'd down the last of my beer from the heavy mug and I'd smash it over his head, just above the brows and then I'd watch him bleed and all the friends and foes would turn to me and they'd say, "Dorothy!" That's what they'd call me and it wouldn't even matter if it was a girl's name or that I lost a testicle falling down the old wooden stairs at Grandma's, hooked my little sack on a nail, the bloody grape just hanging there on that nail painted the same maroon as the stairs, and me bleeding red on the gray concrete floor, howling in the heat of the crackling wood stove and Grandpa at the back of the basement taking a leak in the sump pump, saying "quit yer hollerin'!" The Tigers are on and it's only the top of the fifth and they're down and Grandpa lets me sip from his bottle of Kessler's while he calls nine-one-one. Grandma holds a towel to my groin and she's crying and Mom and Dad will probably be real mad when they get back from their trip. I was supposed to be a good boy, but instead I got a nut torn off.

I was best friends with that Jake in fourth grade and I told him how I only had one nut. The secret just kind of laid dormant for a few years like herpes or chicken pox and scabies, and then in junior high I started getting called names like "Uni" and when I got caught shoplifting cigarettes they started calling me the "one ball bandit." The only person I ever told had been Jake and that's why now I lay in bed most night with my thinks swirling and I kill him in my mind and everything since then that hasn't been quite right suddenly is. And then I wonder about forgiveness and the Bible and Jesus and I feel bad, but then I remember that Jesus got to be the son of God. I'm just the son of Dave Doherty the Roofer. But maybe everybody needs to carry a cross around and be strung up. We just don't see because without knowing what you're looking at it might just be a "T." Think if every time you saw that letter it was a murder. I think that might be true.

Even the roofing guys know about my nut. They're a little better about it, their teasing more out of the fact that I'm my dad's son and they better get their licks in while they can, because in ten years they'll still be climbing ladders with aching, broken spines and I'll be in be inside doing the kind of work they emasculate, because it isn't an option for them.

Maybe one day Jake will apply for a job and I'll call him into the office and we'll joke and enjoy the AC and he'll be wondering the whole time if I remember what he did and I'll let him wonder and I'll let him sweat even though it's seventy-two in my office - mid-nineties on the roof - and I'll give him the job on the condition he doesn't tell anyone about my nut. And then when he hears them call me Uni, Jake will wonder who told and if it'll get back to me.

But right now I'm at the bar, I'm outside and there are no fights to see, no one to interfere with, and I'm left with my swirling thinks in the amber in my glass and I wonder something: "How does a man change?" Is it something as simple as letting time pass? Time has passed and I feel the same. It can't be that easy, can it?

Know Your Enemy

Some people say it's the eyes. Or the way they dance, their balance and all that, are their knees shakin'? Nah, it ain't nothin' like that. That shit, you can train the mad dogs not to blink, show ferocity that ain't. You can force yourself still or dance yourself smooth in front of a mirror. That stuff used to fool me. Put me on edge. Don't no more 'cause I learned about the real place men cut their teeth while they're cuttin' teeth. You want to know how to know who's hard? You want to know if you can take a fool? If he might be a somethin' and not a nothing? It's the knucks. Look at the knuckles when the fool starts talking shit, bobbin and weavin', givin' them crazy eyes. Them knucks clean? They smooth? Well, then he burger.

The Reunion

I watch the child eye the rack of sweet treats.

"Twix." I will at him. "Get a Twix."

He continues eyeing the shining wrappers, glossy and reflecting the florescent banks overhead. It's so impossible to choose. Even if he had all night. Even if he could choose ten of them. And that's why I help him.

"Twix." I say with soft smoky breath. I lick my lip and taste the nicotine on my moustache. He continues to stare, the kid. He's maybe five years old and his mother is looking through the magazines a few aisles down. A man leaves fifty cents on the counter and holds up a daily, no words. I nod. Now it's the three of us in the store. Me and the mom and the kid. Kids shouldn't be forced to make such decisions. Each package crafted by a team of crafty ad men, custom designed to grab the eye, the emotions, pull on heart strings and implant nostalgia. It's so unfair. He is gone. I see it in his eyes. He is gone.

He is gone.

Gone.

"Twix." An earlobe vibrates. Has he heard? Has he listened? His mother flips through a Vogue. She's flipping through Vogue in a gas station. She is getting a lesson in fashion next to the rotation hotdogs, sweaty and red on skewers, dripping orange grease onto stainless steel. She's next to the stale corn chips and hot nacho cheese you pump out with a red lever. It's fall and she's reading about the spring line, the previous spring line, she doesn't know it.

"Joey?" she says.

"Yes, mama?"

"You pick out your candy yet, sweety?"

"I'm looking."

"Twix." I reach above my head and pull a red pack of cigarettes from the elevated rack that lines the whole of the counter. I put them in the pocket of my shirt. The fabric is worn thin and you can read the brand name through the pocket, over my heart. You can read the warning. I do, but I'm not worried. I'm not pregnant.

I watch Joey continue to continue. I watch his mother flip through the glossy pages. I've flipped through that Vogue plenty. It's thick and mostly advertisements. And the stories are really just advertisements too. All the interviews are people who are selling something: clothes, a movie, music. I might sound a little judgmental here behind the counter, elevated eight inches so as to dissuade would be robbers, but I take money the same as them. Put me in a magazine about working in a gas station. I'll answer your questions. Every one of them. Maybe even truthfully. And then I'll suggest you try the hot dogs.

She puts the magazine back, upside down, backwards, in front of Fangoria and says, "Pumpkin head, c'mon, let's go. Daddy's waiting in the Durango." The kid grabs the Twix and I smile and I look at her as she looks at me and eyes me over, wondering what I was looking at her boy so intently for.

I know her. I remember her from school. She was in my class and I remember her in the cafeteria lunch times. I remember her hair was blonder then, bleached out. Now it looks fuller and darker and the tint of gray suits her. Like most the girls back in school, she didn't eat anything at lunch but diet pills, and I think they even threw those up. I remember when she and her friends all got their teeth capped because the vomit acid burned away all the enamel. I remembered thinking those big white chompers of hers were something. All the girls' teeth were, matching bags and matching teeth and matching bleached out hair. I often longed to watch them puke their guts out. It was such a fine ritual, right after lunch. Everyone talked about it and the fat girls were so envious and the boys were so hard for them, thinking of the lengths they could go to for perfection, fake teeth and dry heaves. Laxatives. Imagine the prettiest girls in school all in a row, lining the bathroom stalls, pretty lace panties around their knees, farting like a chorus line and stinking up the place while the fat girls licked their teeth for any remnants of a meal, dreaming of the next one, staring into the mirrors and wishing they were something less.

I smile big and say. "You remember me?"

"How can I forget you, Lloyd?" she says. "I see you here a couple times a week."

"Nah, from school I mean. Remember me from school?"

"High school?"

"Yeah."

"Sure. I guess." She taps the candy bar on the counter. I look at it, put my hands to the keys and I watch her eyes relax. I pull my fingers away and watch her stop breathing.

"You going to the reunion?"

"The class reunion? Is there even going to be one?"

"It's fifteen years. I hope so." I say. I wink at Joey, he's standing tip toes, eyes over the counter, watching his candy, waiting for it to be his. I dance my fingers over the buttons like I'd tap away on the dance floor with his mama given the chance.

"Eighty-nine," I say.

She starts digging through the purse. "And whatever he's got on seven." She throws her head back toward the man in the blue dodge. He looks at me through his glass and through mine. I nod and he looks away. I dip her in my mind.

"Forty-two," I say before adding, "Eighty-nine." I give the boy a wink again and can't see his mouth but his eyes scrunch up and I know he's smiling. I break the fifty and give her the change. She gets to the door and I say, "Gonna put him in your pouch?"

"Excuse me?"

"The boy. You going to put him in your pouch?"

She rolls the words over, "I don't follow."

"He's a Joey. You know? A baby kangaroo?"

She laughs through a breath and it must be getting cold outside because I see the breath as she stands in the open doorway.

"Oh, I get it."

She's gone, dragging the boy behind her and I say, not too loud, "Wasn't a joke, bitch."

I light up my cigarette in the empty store and put the Vogue back where it belongs. I put on some fresh coffee and then sit on the curb runs all along the station. The clouds are rolling in and there's a good chance for some snow. We don't usually get such weather this far down. Might be nice. I wonder if there will be a reunion and if I'll go. My smoking hand is purple and veiny in the cold and the headlights cut the dark and light me up and I know whoever's behind the dark glass of the car at the pump is looking at me and wondering what the hell I'm staring at.

Two Creepers Meet Outside the Elementary School

Hey, man.

Hello.

What the hell you doin'?

Pardon?

What the hell you doin' here?

Are you as cop?

No, but this is my spot.

Oh? I didn't know you had dibs.

Yeah, well I got dibs.

I was being facetious. You can't call dibs. Not on a school.

Look, you can be *fag*cetious all day, but I've been scoping this school for over a week. It's mine.

You should have pounced. You snooze, you lose.

Ha, you snooze, you lose. Look, I'll mess you up if I have to.

First, you couldn't. I run a Tae Kwon Do school. Second, I'll call the cops.

You'll call the cops?

Yeah, I'll call the police.

On me?

On you.

Even though you'd have to expose yourself.

Ha!

What's so funny?

What you just said "expose yourself."

You know what I mean!

I got kids from my class here. Look, this kid left his gi after beginners' last night. I'm just returning it.

Oh, how convenient.

No, I'm smart. You don't have much experience with this, do you?

Hey, I'm plenty experienced.

Yeah right. That your van? Nice windows.

Screw you, man.

Screw me? I'm really starting to question your dedication to this whole scene.

Deep breathe, deep breathe. Look, why don't you just go over to Fifth Street.

To the girls' school? Gross.

Damn. How about St. Joe's?

Catholics? No thanks.

You are a choosy bastard, aren't you?

Look who's talking. You go someplace else.

Okay, okay. I'll give you five hundred bucks to just go away until tomorrow.

What about after tomorrow?

We'll time share it, alternate or days: Monday, Wednesday, Friday one week, Tuesdays and Thursdays the next.

Hm. Where's the five hundred?

Right here. This is my hush money so you know what kind of position you're creating for me.

Okay, but just because I'm a good guy.

Here. There's the bell, there's the bell! Now beat it!

My pleasure.

Freak.

To Sleep Well

She was looking for answers and the pharmacist didn't blink when she bought eight boxes of condoms with a sandwich bag full of change. He counted the coins patiently while the huffing line behind the girl grew.

"Do you want a bag?" he said.

"Um, no."

"You going to carry all these? I think you should have a bag."

"Okay," she said. "Plastic then." And the pharmacist placed the boxes into the crinkling white bag with the receipt. She thanked him. At the exit, the doors opened automatically and she felt like a queen.

She had a man in mind. She saw him most days when her dad drove her to school. He slept under the overpass with the other men and women, but the way he slept, curled into a little ball, oblivious to the trains that rumbled past and the biting flies, he seemed to have a secret and she wanted to know what it was. To sleep well, that was her wish.

She dreamt about him most nights, long before she ever saw him, and then began daydreaming through algebra lessons, feeling her clitoris swell, her tap drip. She excused herself to the restroom often. Rumor was she was pregnant and had the morning sickness. Alone in the restroom stall, her moaning breaths bouncing off the tile, she pushed her button over and over. Oh that man. He slept so well.

"What is your secret?" she would say as she came. "What is it?" And should a different girl be in the next stall, or at the mirror, that other girl would flush and tamp down the secrets no one else knew.

She returned to class glowing, focused on the lesson, but now a distraction to the boys who could, unknowingly, smell the sex on her. The lesson became a scattered, distracted thing as the chalk scraped the board, squeaking and leaving stray white marks like the raised hairs on the necks of all who lived that scene. And the girls saw the attention she drew, from the boys, from the teacher, and those girls hated her, hated her for asking about their secrets.

After dinner she lay on her bed in great anticipation. She showered to pass time and avoided touching herself, avoided the thought of the man and his peaceful sleep. Hair wet, she typed a paper for English class. It was inspired.

She rode her bike in the darkness, passing sleeping houses, the plastic bag crinkling as she peddled. She sweat away her shower and peddled on, breathing heavy, just peddling. She would sleep tonight. Sleep without dreaming, blackness.

She dropped her bike to the ground and approached with caution so as not to step on the sleeping forms scattered atop the dirt. She realized that all of them were sleeping well and she could probably step on each of them without stirring them at all. She pushed away the thought that any one of them would do.

She found him sleeping, curled up and breathing with a congested rattle. She reached out her hand, let it hover over his shoulder, feeling reservation for the first time, not reservation over the act itself, but that it may not work for her in the way she hoped, the way she planned. The man started awake and she jumped back. He sat up, looked at her, his eyes adjusting to the dark.

"Are you real?" he asked. He coughed until he retrieved the stubborn mass. He spit without force of breath and the phlegm stuck to his chin.

She couldn't answer him. She held out the bag and he took it.

He looked inside. "Rubbers? You wanna get fucked? Is that what?"

She nodded and he looked her over. He looked in the bag again. "I got a latex allergy," he said. "I put one of those on and I'll itch for days."

She forced herself to speak. "I thought about that," she said. "There's some latex free in there. Some flavored, big ones, not so big ones."

He looked at her some more and pulled the greasy stub of a cigarette from behind his ear, lit it with a magic match. "This isn't going to help you," he said. "You ain't the first wants my secret."

She bit her lip, held back tears.

"I know what you want." he said. "You want your daddy to come looking for you. You want him to creep into that pink bedroom of yours and find you gone. You want to see him driving that German car on by here, looking for his baby girl. You think he's going to look on over and see you sleeping so well it just couldn't be his girl curled up alongside a man like me and dreaming of all the things that'll never happen to her again. You think that's what he's going to see?" he asked.

She breathed deep, smelling his filth and decay. "I think," she said, "that I have to try. I dream about you nights, even before I saw you. I dreamed of you every night. Don't you dream about me?"

The man sighed, flicked the cigarette away and reached into the plastic bag. "Every night," he said. "Every day."

And she wept as he took her into his hard arms. Face pressed into his chest, she felt the crowd of men and women move around them, closing in, not curious, but duty bound.

Pink Rubber Slivers

Bruce Collins walked the eight blocks home from the bus stop to find his son Michael dancing on top of the car again.

"Michael," Bruce said. Michael's shoes squeaked on the dented hood of the station wagon as he did a series of heel turns. Bruce watched for a moment, mesmerized, not by the moves, but by the familiarity of the scene. He had come home to this so often, it seemed as if he was seeing it now for the first time, as if his old eyes had just now gained some kind of ability to see a hidden underlying form. The problem was, despite the novelty of the observation, he still didn't know what he was looking at. New eyes or no, Bruce's old brain was the same and the insight was fleeting. He turned and saw the old couple, the Joneses, across the street, sitting on their porch swing, rocking back and forth, watching, but not. It was a common sight to everyone on the street, Michael atop the car. Occasionally, the passing traffic would slow to take in the random scene, this teenage boy dancing on the car to whatever music was pumping from the garage sale Sony Walkman clipped to his hip, up through the oversized headphones affixed to his hot ears.

Bruce sighed. He was no longer embarrassed. He was done with that. He left Michael to his dancing and gave a half-hearted wave to the neighbors. To the Joneses it looked less like a wave and more like he was shooing a bug.

Judy was making dinner, warming up a bowl of creamed corn in the microwave while the water, milk, and butter for the potato flakes was starting to boil over. The radio was loud, too loud. Bruce was convinced that these shrill, talk radio jokers operated at some secret frequency that made their words impossible to ignore. He thought maybe he should get some headphones like Michael.

"Hi," he said as he kicked off his loafers and dropped his briefcase. Judy didn't hear him.

"If that's what your mother said," the radio therapist shrieked, "then write her off!"

"Damn straight," Judy said, adding the flakes to the boiling pot.

"How was your day?" Bruce asked.

"But she's my mother," the radio caller said.

"Look, why did you call my show? You wanted my opinion and there you have it. People will try to tear you down and if you don't fight back, they're going to succeed. Understand? I haven't talked to my own mother in over fifteen years! I know what I'm talking about. Don't be a moron!"

"Thanks, Dr. Janice," the caller said. Dr. Janice announced a station break, but before Bruce could register any relief she was back on the airwaves hawking gold investments. Bruce held his breath and looked out the window. There was Michael, still at it, spinning, turning, and jumping new dents into the hood of the wagon. Bruce could complain, but why? The car had been broken down in the driveway for almost a year. Who knew what was wrong with it? It was easier to just take the bus.

Little Judy, LJ they called her, was at the table, her nose in a math book. The kid was six years old, a kindergartener and she was already doing math homework. Damn, was that pre-algebra? Bruce remembered when he was in kindergarten. His report card was nothing but a list of skills each kid needed to progress in to pass into the upper grades, things like zipping a jacket, tying shoes, hopping on one foot, sharing. He was pretty sure he didn't have math in kindergarten, let alone homework.

"LJ," he said. "How was school?"

"It was a vacation day," she said. "Oh, hi, Daddy. Shoot!" LJ took to the paper with a violent fervor, pink rubber slivers of eraser accenting her mistake before she blew them all away.

Bruce grabbed a beer from the refrigerator and sat down on the couch in the dark. He thought about turning on the TV, and looked around for the remote, but it was sitting neatly atop the cable box. He sat in the dark and drank his beer.

Dinner was the sound of the radio punctuated with fork tongs scraping the plates and Michael's footsteps outside. "What the hell keeps him going?" Bruce wondered.

"It's my belief," said Dr. Janice, "that adopted children have no souls."

Bruce looked up from his plate, looked to LJ and then Judy for a reaction. "Is she serious?" he said. "How can she say that? That's horrible."

Judy looked up from her spuds as if he was some swamp creature dropped by unannounced.

"We don't know," Judy said. "She could very well be right."

"Judith," Bruce said. "I was adopted."

Judy shrugged and mixed in a little creamed corn with a forkful of potatoes. "It's just her opinion, Bruce. Everyone's got a right to their opinion." She stood and went to the radio, turned it up louder and sat again. LJ was asleep on her math book, her untouched dinner still lightly steaming next to her head, a thin lock of blonde hair in the corn.

"They work her too hard at that school. It's not even seven and look at her."

"What?" Judy asked.

"It's my opinion," the therapist screamed. "If you don't like it, don't call and ask for it!"

"Nothing," Bruce said. He got up and stroked his daughter's head as he passed, got a streak of creamed corn on his hand for his trouble. He wiped the hand on his khakis and went outside, shutting Dr. Janice inside the house and moving away from the door until she was just barely audible.

"Michael," he said. "Michael, come eat dinner." Michael continued to dance, spinning, shoes squeaking, the hood of the wagon taking a beating. Bruce stepped to the front of the vehicle, his knees feeling the cool bumper. "Michael!" But his presence didn't register. He reached up toward his son, for the headphone connection on top of the Walkman. This act Michael seemed to sense and the boy danced away from his father's hand and threw a couple of half hearted kicks at the open palm. The kicks fit perfectly into the silent rhythm, the weight shifting to the boy's planted leg and thumping out the metallic beat.

Across the street, the Joneses were still on their porch swing, golden in years, and golden under the porch light. Bruce could see the moths attacking the light with stochastic love and confusion. Bruce waved to the couple, but the Joneses just sat swinging back and forth together, unable to see their neighbor through the dark.

Inside, the kitchen was empty. The dishes were cleared, the math book lay open, homework finished and spotted with tiny dried flecks of creamed corn.

"Until tomorrow, I'm Dr. Janice. And that's my opinion." The theme music faded up - a seventies tune he'd once loved - and Bruce twisted the volume dial down until the he heard the merciful click of the dial hitting the off position. He stood still in the kitchen, taking in the muffled denting, the light snoring of LJ in her room, the running water of Judy's evening bath. He grabbed another beer from the refrigerator and half sat in front of the TV before remembering the remote and grabbing it. He turned on the news and drank his beer. The light of the TV flickered blue with every new shot, lighting up the dark room like a broken strobe light at a party for one.

Bruce woke up when the TV went black. He startled from a POV dream where he was riding a bicycle down a hill he'd never seen, but knew well. Faster and faster he'd gone, unable to stop, but equally unable to desire stasis, and then he was falling, pissing himself, and crashing awake into his life, warm beer soaking his lap. Michael stood behind him with the remote.

"Hey, Pop. You fell asleep. Long day?"

"It was alright," Bruce said. "How was school?"

"Was a holiday," Michael said. "For us anyway, teachers had to go in. Oh, the Joneses told me our porch light burned out."

"Oh, thanks Joneses."

"Right. They're kind of funny, huh? Always on that swing."

"I suppose we're all a bit funny."

Michael seemed to think about that for a bit. "I'm going to bed, Pop. Goodnight."

"Do your homework?"

"Oh yeah, math, it's done," he said.

"Good night, Son."

Bruce got a light bulb from the utility room and went outside. He unscrewed the old bulb and shook it, listening to broken filament bounce against the glass. He screwed in the new bulb and the light glowed yellow, soft. Bruce looked across the street. The Joneses had gone inside and everything was quiet on the street. He put the old bulb in his pocket.

Bruce stood on the Joneses' porch, looking at his own house, at the broken down car in the drive, at the moths swirling around his own porch light. The Joneses' house was completely dark inside. They were no doubt asleep. Bruce wondered what he would do when he was retired, when his kids were grown and gone like Sam and Gladys Joneses' were. Bruce sat down on their swing, rocked back and forth lightly, listened to the rattle of the chain and the dry metal on metal squeak of the hook and eye loop above.

Bruce stopped at the station wagon, ran his hand over the dented hood. Maybe he should get it fixed. He'd now spent more on bus fair than it would have cost to fix the car, probably, he didn't know. He was going to go in when he saw the Walkman on the hood of the car. He picked it up and put the headphones on. He pushed play and the world went silent. Bruce climbed on the car, closed his eyes and dance. He spun like his son had, felt the give of the hood under his feet. He danced and danced until he was sweat glazed in the muggy night. No one saw him, but he didn't care if they did. He continued to move and sweat, taken away by his own movement.

Bruce was completely lost when his foot caught a collection of his perspiration and he slipped, stumbled back, catching himself on the edge of the hood, flapping his arms, willing himself forward, but falling back. He didn't panic. He smiled with the knowledge that he was on the cusp of something bigger than any place fear dared live.

I Hope It's True What They Say about Cats

I met them at the Houdini, that magic themed bar off of Las Vegas Boulevard. You know the place. The wait staff is a mix of wannabe magicians and wannabe something elses, people who'd learned a few sleight of hand tricks and now wondered how to make their prospects reappear.

They were visiting from Ohio. They bummed my Parliaments and let me pick up the tab. The girl danced to a swamp rock tune on the juke while her man fed quarters into the Zoltar fortune teller until he got a card he could live with. He showed it to her. She continued to sway in her fringed leather vest and oversized shades while she read the words on the card. He came back to the bar, put down the stack of fortunes. I read them.

> What's vice today may be virtue tomorrow
> You are fortunate in pursuits of the heart
> The best way to defeat an enemy is to make a friend
> Your joyful heart ignites the love of those around you
> Regret is merely a gentle prod in the right direction. Move on

We left the bar together, back onto the strip. It was dark but for the glow of the city, just another lonely star. We passed the Mirage, the Venetian, got redirected through construction to the Harrah's complex and then jaywalked in front of Caesar's. We played penny slots at Bill's and lost and drank watered-down beer. I followed them again, through crowded sidewalks, past the strange collection of souls. Las Vegas was a great equalizer, the only place to see a Holocaust survivor and a frat boy communing over gin drinks while the dealer stood on seventeen and still managed to bust them both.

Nearly every homeless person we saw had a cat. Cats on leashes, cats with sunglasses, cats that looked dead. The only one who didn't have a cat had a guitar. I put a dollar in his coffee can and whispered a song and he played it. My new friends danced and I watched the passersby step around them.

We entered their hotel through the casino and she lost her last five dollars on a horse whose name she liked. We took the elevator to the top floor where they said they had a suite. He pulled out a key and unlocked the door labeled "Roof Access- Maintenance Personnel Only."

"How'd you get that?" I asked.

"Found it," he said. "Stroke of luck."

I stood with her man and we looked over the edge of the building, tiny and pathetic things below. She pulled me by the hand, away from him, away from the wind.

"You're not alone," she said.

"She left me for a magician."

"Magic isn't real," she said.

She kissed my cheek, thanked me for the cigarettes and joined her man at the edge of the building. They didn't touch, didn't speak. They just took a moment to look out over the city lights.

Just Running

As soon as I walked in the door I heard Tina crying - no, I knew before that. I could smell her tears like sea air and I knew it had something to do with Millie, it always did. Tina was at the table, smoking a cigarette while another burned in the ashtray. She always did that and it drove me nuts. I didn't smoke anymore - my heart - and though I didn't mind the second-hand smoke or the stale smell on everything in the house, I hated that little quirk. I hated it because it was something.

She was drinking brandy from one of the gold-rimmed snifters we kept next to the bottles in the cabinet. If the crying was about the dog or from the brandy, I couldn't say. We'd been together thirty-two years so I didn't know her at all.

"Millie," she said, "she ran away!"

"She didn't run away. She's just running."

"That asshole lawn kid left the gate open again. He only thought to tell me when he came for the check."

"Did you pay him?"

"Of course I did!" She drank. "What kind of question is that? Millie is probably on the side of the road somewhere."

"Easy. I'll find her."

"Now?"

"Yes, now. Let me change my shoes at least, huh?"

I went to the spare bedroom and found my old white sneakers and used my heels to slide off my wing tips. I slid the sneakers on and almost took them off again to change my socks, but the way Tina was sniffling I knew I'd hear it if I didn't move. I grabbed a beer and put it in the inside pocket of my jacket, grabbed another and cracked it. I drank in long cold swallows and left the house. Tina wasn't crying anymore. She was lighting another cigarette.

I walked the bank of the shallow creek, not knowing if it was even the right way. It was the way I went the last time and that was all I knew. Millie was a Cairn, a little Toto terrier and she was a little cunt. I'd taken a small moment of delight when Tina had said, "on the side of the road". Millie was sweet when she was a puppy, but as soon as she went into her first heat she had a false pregnancy and never came out of it. Most often my shoes served as her litter and the first time it happened, I reached down to grab them and she bit my hand without warning. I kicked the shit out of her and Tina screamed and I screamed and showed her my bleeding hand. Millie ran off and did a shit on the bed. We took her to the vet and the lady suggested spaying, but Tina wouldn't have it. She had a dog when she was a kid. It went in for a spay job and never came out of anesthesia, so I was relegated to fighting for my shoes whenever Millie found them, fighting with our goddamn dog. It was embarrassing.

I finished the first can of beer and dropped it into the nearly dry creek bed. I cracked the other and as soon as it hit my lips I wished for a third.

"Millie!" I yelled. "Millie!" I listened to fall, the crinkling brown leaves on the cooling wind. I walked.

There were a couple boys playing in a standing pool of water, netting minnows. I thought about my girls. I used to take them on walks this way when they were kids. Now they were grown and gone and I rarely saw or heard from them unless they needed me, or money. I missed and loved them like crazy.

"Hey," I said. The boys looked up quick, startled and guilty looking, cigarettes dangling from chapped lips. They mistook me as some kind of authority.

"You see a little dog, wheaten colored?"

"What's wheaten?" One boy asked.

"Golden. Like wheat? You seen her?"

They looked at each other and then back at me and shook their heads. I stood there for a moment looking at them, watching their cigarettes burn.

"That's a hard habit to give up," I said.

"You want one?"

I sipped my beer, shrugged. "Yeah, give me one of those."

The boy closest pulled out a red pack and handed over a cigarette and a plastic lighter. I lit it, sucked deep and coughed. The boys laughed at me. I left them to the minnows.

I found her just as I was wondering what I was going to tell Tina when I came home without the dog. She was panting on the side of the creek, bleeding, tore up from muzzle to gut. I had to guess she'd found a big muskrat or raccoon, maybe another dog. She didn't look at me at all, just laid and panted and bled. I reached down for her and only later thought about her possibly biting me. I unzipped my jacket and tucked her inside. I held her close and stroked her through the fabric as we walked. She was shaking and as her blood leaked through my shirt onto my skin it warmed me.

The Guy from Craigslist

We found a guy on Craigslist who unhaunted houses for fifty dollars.

"I see things," she said. "Invisible things."

The guy yawned, scratched his chin. "Got the money?"

"Thirty," I said, "all we have."

He laughed. "Kids, they'll take it all, even from the grave."

She cried and I held her.

"So, what do you use? Like a vacuum or crucifix or something?"

"Nah, none of that. Ready? Look at me. You, girly, quit crying and look at me."

We did.

"There's no such thing as ghosts. You're both fucking morons."

She and Him

Sam scraped a black and blue fingernail over the smooth surface of the bar. The nail had been pinched in one of the doors at the prison a couple days earlier. He was lucky he was only going to lose the nail. He'd come to losing the whole finger in the door jamb, pulling it free just before the snip.

"See this?" he asked the bartender.

"See what?" Dana asked. Sam was in a few nights a week and it always seemed to be during her shift. She tried to make busy when he was there.

* * *

She stacked the dry glass with the others and reluctantly moved in close to him, looked at his finger.

"Asshole at work nearly tore it off. Shut the door on it."

"Sam, that's disgusting," she said, ignoring his wandering eyes.

She was used to guys checking out her tits and ass at every opportunity, but Sam repulsed her. It wasn't that he was bad-looking. He was well built and impeccably groomed - a necessity when working at the prison, she figured. Dana really couldn't give a reason she disliked him – well, she could, but a single finger wouldn't cover it, a palm wouldn't cover it. It was his casual racism, like when he asked if "that Gook" was in the kitchen without a hint of embarrassment when she told him Bruce was Chinese, not Vietnamese.

"Can't even tell them apart," he'd said, as if his own ignorance was evidence of some universal truth. But Sam wasn't just a racist, but he was also sexist to a misogynistic degree, and a homophobe. But he was also a regular and that meant money for the café. And in a way, Dana liked having him around to offend her sensibilities. It made her realize she hadn't yet hit rock bottom with men.

Robert walked up, smiling until he saw Sam. "Dana, I need a gin and tonic for that sweetie over on thirteen."

Sam looked over his shoulder and saw her. She was alone at the small table, dressed in a white summer dress, thin straps over tan shoulders, brown hair tucked behind her ears. She looked like a tomboy trying to dress to impress. It worked for her.

"And for some reason she wants to buy a round for this growth on your bar," Robert said, thumbing to Sam. Sam vaguely caught the insult, but was too smitten to care.

"Really?" he asked, hopefully.

"Really?" Dana asked, incredulously.

"Really," Robert conceded. He shook his head and walked away.

Dana began mixing the drink, starting with the hand-squeezed lime juice then adding a shot of Tanqueray gin and the tonic water. Sam continued to stare.

"Let me bring her the drink, huh?" he said to Dana. She put the gin and tonic and another lager in front of him. He breathed into his hand and sniffed, grabbed the drinks. Robert stopped in front of him, carrying a plate of oysters.

"Piece of advice," Robert said. "Don't talk."

"Fuck you," Sam said lightly.

"Just sayin'."

Sam stepped past Robert and again set his eyes on the sweet thing by the window, haloed by the lamplight outside.

She saw him approach and smiled. She had broken another of Mom's rules: a woman never pursues. But she couldn't help herself when she saw Sam at the bar. He was just as handsome as she remembered from high school. She'd had such a crush on him back then, but had no chance. Now however, she'd been around, learned things about style, like that she was actually a spring, not a winter. She'd learned how to make up her eyes to best make her baby blues pop and to match it with the perfect complimentary shade of lipstick. She wondered if he'd remember her at all. She'd had some work done, but nothing he couldn't see through if he looked closely enough. And then she thought about the boy Kevin from school, the one Sam had beaten the shit out of after one of the football games. She doubted he remembered Kevin; however, if she mentioned "Fag Boy" she was pretty sure he'd recall. Why she was still attracted to him was beyond her, but she'd long ago given up on searching out the psychology of longing, desire. Desires just *were*.

Sam stopped at the edge of the table, drinks in hand. She looked at him. He had no words. He imagined he was still at the bar, watching this pathetic version of himself and yelling: *don't fuck this up like everything else!*

"Is that mine?" she asked, sensing his unease. It was cute.

Sam nodded, smiled.

"Can I have it?" she asked.

"Yeah, of course, sorry." Sam set the drink down, spilling a bit over the side of the glass. He wished he'd taken a shot or two. He sipped his beer.

"Thanks for the round," he said wiping foam from his lip with the back of his hand.

"My pleasure," she said. "Want to join me?" She could hear Mom: *A lady doesn't ask a man to join her. She lets him ask.*

Sam sat across from her and took another drink. She dabbed at the spill with her napkin and then sipped her drink through the red swizzle straw.

"So," he said. "What brings you to Machiasport?"

"I'm from here actually. I just got back into town. I was in college, and then Thailand for the last year teaching English. Going back in a couple months."

"Wow, that's sounds exciting," he said. "I'd like to travel, but I'm pretty busy with work." *But not to a country full of chinks.*

Robert walked by carrying two slices of key lime pie.

"What do you do?" she asked, eyeing the pie. *He works at the prison. Like all the townie boys.*

"I work at the prison."

"Isn't it scary? All those violent men in one place?"

"Isn't so bad. Want to see something?"

"Okay."

He held up the finger he'd smashed.

"Oh," she winced.

"This is about the worst I've been hurt on the job, caught it in a door."

"Does it hurt?"

"Nah." He said. He looked at her. Her eyes held him captive, lost in the forest of her lashes. "I can't believe I haven't seen you before."

"I've seen you," she said.

"Where?"

"Around," she said. She hoped she was coming off coy, not cold. Mom said a lady should act so a man can just barely tell the difference, enough to keep him interested while also keeping him at a distance.

He tried to place her. Their silence hung heavy and the café noise seemed to swell, the clinking of forks on plates, chewing, the cacophonic hum of the conversations. Sam downed his beer and set it down hard on the table. She jumped.

"Sorry, sorry." He breathed deeply. "Look, I'm terrible at this kind of thing, so I'm just going to be honest. I think you are about the most beautiful creature I've ever seen."

She smiled. He relaxed a bit.

"I mean it. You want to go out with me sometime? Man, I wish you'd been around for Margaretta Days. I would have loved to take you. But..."

She looked at him and he was afraid she was searching for some excuse. God, he hated himself - too eager, idiot! His face flushed and he felt like everyone in the place was looking at him.

"Margaretta Days, they still do the reenactments?" She rolled her eyes. "I used to play a fur trapper."

"I used to be a Redcoat."

"No kidding?"

"I wouldn't kid about Margaretta Days." He circled the rim of his mug with the bruised finger. "You still didn't answer my question."

She nodded, smiled into her lap. "I'd like that. But I think we should do something else first." She met his eyes and leaned in. "I want you to take me into the bathroom and fuck me. And then I want to eat a piece of the amazing key lime pie they have here."

Sam sat stupid. "Excuse me?"

"You heard me. Take me into the bathroom and fuck me. Then buy me a piece of pie."

Stand up, you moron!

Sam stood quickly, knocking the table with his knee and held out his hand. She took it and he led her past the tables, past Dana and Robert talking at the bar.

They hit the men's room door and he led her in, took her to the handicapped stall. Her large hands were on the tile, fingers spread wide like her legs.

"Lift the dress and fuck my ass. Now."

Sam unbuckled his belt, snagging his bad nail on it. The nail pulled away from the bed and began to bleed. Sam lifted the dress and sucked the blood from his finger.

She squealed. Mom didn't have a rule to cover this situation, but she'd hardly approve. It felt so good, but she didn't know if it was his cock, or Sam. Did she want him for him, or a trophy? And what was he going to say when she told him her secret over pie, about returning to Thailand for one last procedure? No matter what happened, Kevin never felt more like a woman than she did with Sam in her ass, even while cursing her inevitable erection.

A Bottle Room Can Save a Marriage

Dad taught math at the high school for almost thirty years before a student finally sporked him to death in the cafeteria. He bled out right there on the floor. Thirty cell phones recorded the scene, but no one thought to call 911.

I was at college when it went down, and if I have the timeline right, I was getting fucked in the ass when it happened, first time. It's funny, me and Dad both bleeding out of holes on opposite ends at the same time. I guess true opposites would have been say, his neck and my feet, but Davey Braddock wasn't going to fuck my feet. I'd have let him though. Some people are into that.

The bottle room used to be this little room where we had an electric train set up on top a broken ping pong table. We sculpted mountains out of chicken wire and paper mache, painted them rocky brown and textured them with plastic pine trees, painted little buildings and the tiny model people. The train set was up for about a week before Dad threw a fit and smashed it all to shit after he couldn't paint a smile on one his people. He said the brush was "fucked," that he was "fucked."

At first it was just Dad, he'd finish a bottle and smash it against the wall of the train room, the shards of glass like an icy winter storm blowing through our little town. Dad and Mom yelled at each other a lot less after that and even though I woke up at least three nights a week to the sound of smashing glass, it was better than hearing them say they were going to kill each other. Neighbors didn't call the police anymore, and in bed I cried and jerked off to the sound of breaking glass, so happy to live in a normal family, finally.

Me and my little sis and Mom, we started smashing bottles in the room too. And after a time, not just bottles, but any kind of glass that needed disposing: big pickle and applesauce jars, spaghetti sauce jars, light bulbs. We switched from cans and plastic bottles of Coke to Mexican horchata and pineapple soda, just for the glass. We couldn't get enough. Even friends of me and my little sis started bringing over glass. They'd walk through the door and put their toll into the recycle box and Dad's ears would perk up as he sat in his chair in front of the television, sucking down another bottle, finally in possession of a noble purpose beyond forgetting. Dad even got rid of the old light fixtures and put in buzzing fluorescent banks throughout the house. We all squealed and cheered as the long tubes burst and popped like lady fingers. We watched one another, happy, the live bulbs painting our teeth green and exposing every flawed inch of skin as we loved like a family should love and made memories worth keeping.

We went on a family drive every Sunday, stopped at every tavern in a twenty mile radius, my sis and me digging through the dumpsters and collecting every bottle, running the ones with liquor inside straight back to Dad. He polished them off while he and Mom sat quiet on the hood of the car. They watched us, arms around one another, swaying to mellow hits of the seventies on AM radio, the music crisp and clear and tinny through the car speakers. Then, smiling, my sis and I climbed back into the dumpsters, fighting off the raccoons and rats for the prizes. There were so many prizes, so many treasures. And we found them all.

The bottle room was kept closed unless we were smashing. The smell inside was sweet and rank and it attracted fruit flies, but each smash night Dad used his hard shoulder to force the door open, his grunts and the sound of glass shards sliding over the shredded carpet gave voice to our anticipation. Night after night this happened and it got to where Dad needed my help with the door because there was so much glass inside, and then Mom's help, and then little sis. We should have expected it, but eventually we couldn't budge the door given all the glass wedged beneath it. We looked to Dad for a solution, but it was like the stuck door turned something off inside him. He looked us over and it was like he was seeing the door and us for what we were, an ephemeral distraction from a hard truth. And just that quickly, it was all over. The rest of it continued for me and Mom and sis, the collecting, the Sunday road trips, but the room stayed closed and the glass filled the garage and the staircase and the hallways, and more and more often I was woken up by the sound of screams and threats and tears. I'd masturbate to the memories of smashing glass and wish to hell my own piece would just crack off in my hand so I could throw it through my window and jump out and run away forever. It seemed like such a real possibility, but the futility of such a wish dawned on me as I shamed into my stiff sock.

I watch the videos from time to time, alone with whatever boy is snoring next to me on my futon. I watch on my laptop in the dark, watch my dad there bleeding, that white spork sticking out of his neck and I wonder if he was thinking about me and my sis and Mom. Did he have any regrets? I hope he didn't, but I know better. Was he scared? I hope he wasn't. He made us happy sometimes.

The Night I Dug up Raymond Carver

When Ray Carver came back from the dead, the first thing he said was, "God Damn there's a lot of zombie shit these days." And then he got quiet, reflective. He looked at me and said, "They *are* zombies right? Not a bunch of lepers or something?"

"Yes, zombies," I assured him. He started searching his pockets for the forgotten things. He had a lighter. It didn't work, no fluid. He opened and closed it, not seeming to mind that it was useless.

"Coming back to life is like coming back to a place you haven't seen in a long, long time."

He said everything was familiar, just not immediately.

"So, what do you want to do?" I asked. I felt self-conscious. I dug him up. I should have had a plan.

"What I really want to do is bury myself," he said.

"Oh," I said. Or something equally inane. I have no ear for dialogue.

He smiled. "In some fucking pussy!"

* * *

Ray took me to this place he knew in Vegas, not flashing Vegas, but one of the dark places. The club was gray wood against the sky and you could hear the termites eating their way inside. You could see the strip, a low glow in the distance. But this wasn't there. The marquee board on the curb was a far cry from the Paris balloon or the Bellagio fountains. This sign belonged in front of the VFA, advertising a Boy Scout spaghetti dinner fundraiser. But the sign's light was without competition, and it insisted upon itself. It told us in bold block letters that "YOU CAN DREAM TONIGHT OR YOU CAN GO TO BED." Or that's what I made out of "Y U C EAM GHT OR Y O C N GO   BED."

I told myself to write that down.

I never did.

The man at the door of Kitty Cat Club, he was big and black and a mean motherfucker wrapped in silver shark skin. His eyes said he didn't play, but Ray melted his heart with a twenty spot and he showed us his gold fronts.

It was dark upstairs, clouded with cigaret smoke. But the girls' fuck-me-sauce smelled amazing. The place was nearly empty and the available girls flocked to us like pigeon to seed. Not pigeons, but a flock of beautiful birds, vultures maybe? And if that's what they were, I knew what I must have been. Ray didn't give a fuck about any of that.

"Now's not the time," he said to himself. And he turned back to the drink that was already waiting for him when he sat down at the bar.

He threw the occasional bill onto the stage and scratched at the bar. I watched him, the way he stared into his glass. I wished I could love something that much.

He read my mind, gave me a pity glance and said, "It's just words. As many as you want to put down. The secret is knowing which ones to get rid of."

"You want a dance?" the girl asked me, the most recent in a long stream. She had almond eyes and dark island skin. She was wearing an orange and blue flowered lei that matched her bikini.

"No, thanks," I told her.

"Yes he does. Give him one on me." Ray didn't look up from the bar as he pulled the wad of bills from his pocket. All around us, the girls' ears pricked up as they ground themselves into their sad perches.

He gave her two hundred dollars and she led me by the hand, down the stairs and into a hallway I'd missed on the way in. Curtains lined the middle of the wide hall, dividing it in half, sections of fabric that might have been black or purple in the light. The curtains were a fourth wall for a series of small, floor to ceiling particle board rooms. It reminded me of a childhood hideout, even more so when she handed the wad of bills to our angry friend from the door. He put the wad in his mouth, between his cheek and gold teeth. His tongue flicked at each of the bills as he counted them.

The island girl sat me on small couch. The cushion caught me, gave me the slightest foreshadow of security before allowing my ass to crash on the concrete floor.

"Oh yeah," she said. "That one." It was a genuine warning, just delivered too late.

I asked her what two hundred dollars was worth.

"A laugh," she said.

Then she danced for me and I watched her lei move back and forth around her neck, covering her breasts, moving separate from her, but because of her. The lei was all I could really see in the black light of the room. Like the shell of the club itself, her skin was a shade too dark to distinguish itself from the background. She rode my lap like a ghost.

* * *

Ray was not at the bar when I returned. The girls all gathered around me. One by one they passed in front of me and I read the message scrawled on each of their backs, across their shoulders. They crossed in front of me, lifting their glittered hair, each one's perfume mixing with their sweat and marking them like a fingerprint. I read:

> I went to another place. Maybe London
> Where I think about her often.
> She's like a drink in my hand
> cold
> and when she warms up
> she's not as satisfying, but she still has my number so
> don't be surprised when I don't answer.
> Whatever the call.
> You didn't build that fire yourself, Boy
> Isn't that wild?
> All experience. No gift.

"What does mine say?" Each of the girls wanted to know, twisting their necks like owls, chasing their own bodies, dizzy for understanding.

"I don't know," I said. "But I think you got the order confused."

* * *

I waited outside the club, stayed near the door. Cars passed. Men called me names.

"C'mon you fuckers," I whispered when they were gone.

When she appeared she looked the same. Her face blended in with the wall of the club. She's traded her glitter for glasses, dark skin for jeans and sneakers. Her hair is tame north of her hair tie, wild and flowing beyond the noose. She still wore the lei.

"Good. You waited."

"You know where he is?" I asked.

"Who?"

"Ray? The guy I came in with?"

"That's his name? He never told me. I thought it was Chuck."

"It's Ray," I said.

"You sure?"

* * *

We walked to where the road stopped, hopped the barbwire and entered the desert. The air was cold and the stars mocked me, their distant fires were impotent, unable to fix the cold air. I wanted to ask why he was out here, where she was leading me. Instead, I watched thin Brahman cattle graze on the scrub.

"My brother," she said. "He died in the desert. He was after a coyote that killed our dog. He died of thirst. When they found him, his skin was crispy and black from the sun. What the vultures had left anyway."

"I'm sorry," I said.

She laughed. "The coyote didn't kill the dog. I did. I nuzzled in its fur and bit its throat."

She looked at me for the first time since we left the road. Her teeth shone in the moonlight and they looked capable of chewing through anything.

"He wasn't bad," she said. "Who hasn't done something to deserve death?"

"Me," I said.

She laughed. "You lie. Your heart knows. And that's why it wants to stop beating. But it can't because it's a slave to your lesser brain. It can't outsmart the part of you that lies."

I wanted to argue, but I knew she was right either way, in my mind or in hers. The truths led to the same place.

"Is he really out here?" I asked.

"You mean: are you a dog?"

"Yes."

"You see that fire?"

I looked, strained, and in the distance I did see the smallest fallen star, burning, fusing atoms, releasing enough heat to power my heart indefinitely.

"That's him?" I asked.

She didn't answer. She just laughed again.

Trust is expensive. Much more than two hundred dollars.

Maybe it was Ray at the fire, writing stories in the cold earth with a stick. Stories about bars and women and drinks. Stories about donuts and champagne and cigarettes. Stories of men on roofs, chucking rocks. Stories about shy, pretty girls, their heads caved in with different rocks.

We got closer. I saw the dark form crouched in front of the fire. I felt the heat. And the light, it was as blinding as the dark.

"What's he doing?" I said.

"Donuts and champagne," she told me. I didn't see the significance at first. But when I did, years later, I was unable to make the connection back to that night in the desert. It just ate away at me. Like Ray with the donuts.

The Men I Am

I'm afraid of men who look me in the eye. I steer clear and think of the things I'd like to do to them, when I can get the better of them in the dark. I use blunt things to pummel them to sleep. I suck out those eyes and eat them like oysters. I feel them looking at my insides, the oyster eyes, and I wonder where the light comes from, the light they use to see every inside inch of me. I watch the eyeless heads as their eyes watch my stomach churn from the inside, the opening and closing of sphincters as they're shunted through and finally out of my life. Each of these eyes I shit into the bowl. I take a picture and put it on my blog. I do this every day because I carry the collective delusion: if it came from me it must be worth something.

I have eighty-four followers, mostly acquaintances from my home town.

CS DeWildt is a liar. He wants to hurt you. He is the author of the novella *Candy and Cigarettes*, and his work has appeared in a variety of print and web zines. Please visit at csdewildt.com.

www.ingramcontent.com/pod-product-compliance
Lightning Source LLC
Chambersburg PA
CBHW071318130626
46556CB00004B/1653